RED ROVER

Book Two of the Red Series

Red Rover, Red Rover, send someone over.
A traditional children's game now being played by adults.

RED ROVER

Leonard Di Gregorio

Cover designed by Cover Designer: Photo from Shutterstock by Volodymyr Goinyk

This book is a work of fiction. Names, characters, places, and incidents either are products of the author's imagination or are used fictitiously. Any resemblance to actual persons, living or dead, events, or locales is entirely coincidental.

Leonard Di Gregorio
Visit my website at www.LDiGregorio.com

Printed in the United States of America

First Printing: June 2019
Bailey-Webster Publishing

ISBN: 978-1-7331917-0-8

This book is dedicated to my brother Sonny, who always believed in me and inspires me every day.

Sal (Sonny) Di Gregorio
July 10, 1950 – December 16, 2011

ACKNOWLEDGMENT

I want to acknowledge the support of my wife, Barbara, and my two wonderful daughters, Danielle and Michelle, whose support was invaluable in finalizing this manuscript.

A special thank you to Roger Quinn, mentor, and friend, who led me on this path. I never thought I would take.

Thank you, Rich Gale, my story editor, for your patience and guidance.

To my classmates at Coastal Carolina University's Osher Lifelong Learning Institute, and my other editors, for taking time out of their busy schedules to edit this book.

And of course, my beta readers, Caroline (Tinker) Frazier, and Kathy Hughes, who made me look good.

CONTENTS

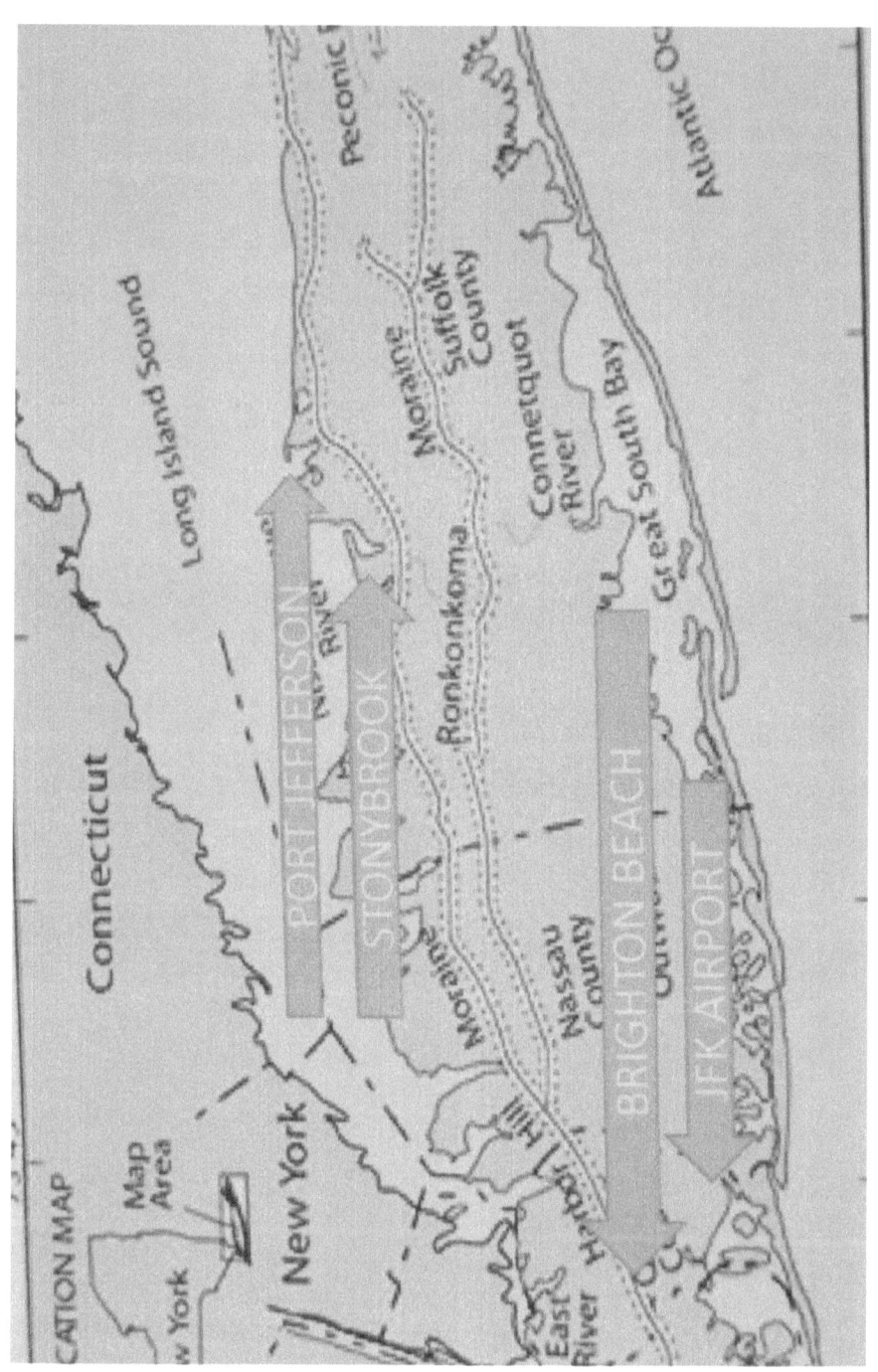

PROLOGUE

Port Jefferson, New York

Sunday, early morning, Port Jefferson, New York. Stepan Bondar parked his red Toyota Tundra pickup on the street across from 60 Laurel and ran up the steps. Jeff Flynn's black Ford F150 was parked in the driveway, a metallic lime green Kawasaki Jet Ski Ultra 310LX on a trailer hitched to its rear.

Jeff opened the door.

"It's about time you showed up. I've been itching to get on the water before the winter."

"Wow! It's gorgeous. When did you get this one?"

"Last week, I traded my 2010 for this one. It's only a 2014, but what a difference! Wait until we get on the water."

"So, what's holding you up? Let's go." Stepan responded.

They jumped into the truck. Jeff expertly backed the vehicle with the trailer out of the driveway.

It took only ten minutes to traverse the roads down to the Port Jefferson boat ramp.

There was a cloudless autumn blue sky with a slight wind blowing across the harbor, causing the waters to be somewhat choppy.

"What a great day for a trip on the sound," beamed Stepan.

"Yeah," confirmed Jeff. "Back the truck up, and I'll launch the jet ski."

Stepan eased the Ford pickup down the ramp, guiding the trailer.

"OK, that's good."

Jeff unclamped the tie-down straps and mounted the personal watercraft. One turn of the key, and he took off. He did a short spin around the harbor and returned to the ramp.

Meanwhile, Stepan pulled the truck up, parked it, and ran back to the ramp to the waiting watercraft.

"Jump on and let's rock and roll," urged Jeff.

"This is great!" yelled Stepan, "I can't believe it's the end of September and it's almost 80 degrees."

"Let's make the most of it before it gets back into the forties," Jeff shouted back.

They traveled out into the harbor passing the old Port Jefferson power plant smokestacks. Silver crystals shimmered off the waves. Seagulls swooped down upon them, calling for their morning's morsels. The Port Jefferson Ferry was returning from Bridgeport with its commuters and tourists. Moments later, they passed the jetty and headed out into Long Island Sound.

Light waves allowed the jet ski to jump slightly, but not as much as they would have liked.

They were out for about thirty minutes when they noticed a yacht in the distance.

"Look at that yacht! I wish we had one instead of this little thing," observed Stepan.

The large white yacht was coming their way. The pilot was sitting atop the flying bridge.

Jeff turned the throttle back, slowing down and making circles waiting for the yacht to pass.

"Look! It must be over fifty feet."

"She's hauling ass. Going about forty knots. Should make some great wakes. Hang on," exclaimed Jeff.

Suddenly, the jet ski stalled. Jeff tried to restart it, but it would not catch.

"What's wrong?" Stepan asked.

"It won't start," answered Jeff, cranking the starter again to no avail.

"Did we run out of gas?"

"No, I just filled it this morning. But I haven't used it in a while. There must have been some water in the line."

"Well, how the hell are we going to get back?"

"I'll wave down the yacht. It can tow us back to the dock."

They both started flailing their arms in the air. Sure enough, the yacht saw their distress signal and headed towards them. It picked up speed as it got closer.

"He'd better slow down, or he'll capsize us," observed Jeff.

"I can see the pilot on the boat. He looks familiar," shouted Stepan.

Suddenly, the yacht turned.

"He's heading for us. I see the pilot looking straight at us. Can't he see us?" Jeff yelled.

"That's…" was the last word Stepan said.

No sooner were the words were spoken when the horrendous sound of two bodies of fiberglass colliding together filled the air.

Stepan and Jeff flew off the jet ski. Jeff hit his head against the side of the yacht and was knocked unconscious. Thankfully his life jacket kept him afloat.

Stepan was thrown into the water. He tried to swim away, but the yacht turned toward him. Once again, he was hit by the boat and dragged under. There was no sign of Stepan as he disappeared under the stern.

The yacht stopped. A dinghy was lowered, and the pilot of the boat, Pavio Kravets, climbed in and retrieved Jeff. There was no sign of Stepan. Back at the yacht, the pilot hooked up the dinghy and hoisted it on board, with Jeff still in it. He placed Jeff on the deck. Blood oozed from his forehead. Pavio went into the cabin. He returned a few moments later with some towels and wrapped them around Jeff's head. He returned to the cabin.

The pilot of the yacht was Pavio Kravets, a little over six feet tall and around 220 pounds, with black slicked-back hair, and wearing tan slacks and blue low-cut tennis sneakers. His biceps fit tightly into the sleeves of his short-sleeved linen shirt. There was a black tattoo partly exposed on his neck and others along both forearms. He marched into the cabin and began the Channel 16 Mayday call in a strong Russian accent.

"Mayday-Mayday-Mayday. This is Lyresa-Lyresa-Lyresa M149325 Mayday! This is Lyresa. Port Jefferson Harbor bearing 185 degrees magnetic, distance 2 miles. Struck by personal watercraft, one person missing, one person injured, unconscious. Need medical attention. Lyresa is a fifty-foot yacht, white hull. Over."

"Coast Guard cutter *John Henry* on the way starting search and rescue. Sending medical helicopter. Please advise any changes. Estimated time of arrival thirty minutes," responded the medical dispatcher. "Secure all loose items on deck."

"Lyresa! Suffolk County Police Marine patrol boat on the way. Estimated time of arrival ten minutes. 10-4, dispatched."

CHAPTER ONE

The Investigation

Fifteen minutes passed. The police boat appeared in the distance, speeding toward the yacht.

As it closed in on the yacht, Pavio noticed the two police officers. The police boat pulled alongside, and Sergeant Mike Foster of the Suffolk County Marine Police called out.

"Did you make a distress call for police assistance?"

"Yes, please come aboard, officer."

Sergeant Foster climbed aboard the yacht and noticed Jeff lying unconscious on the deck. He knelt beside him and checked his pulse and breathing. A small amount of blood was seeping through the towel Pavio had placed on his forehead.

"He's breathing. The medical helicopter will be here any minute."

Sergeant Foster called out to his partner on the police boat, "Frank, hand me the emergency kit and search the area for the missing person, while I attend to this one. And, while you're at it, call the station and have them notify search and rescue. "

"Got it," answered the second officer as he passed over the kit, then sped away.

Sergeant Foster looked at Pavio and noticed bloodstains on his pants and shirt. "Do you have any injuries?"

"No, it's his," answered Pavio as he pointed to the injured man on the deck.

The Sergeant opened the kit and wrapped a pressure dressing around Jeff's head. Then he felt around Jeff's body and located his driver's license and boating license in a waterproof packet. He pulled out the license and entered the information on his notepad: Jeff Flynn, age 32, red hair, 6 foot, 185 pounds, 60 Laurel, Port Jefferson, New York.

Second victim: unknown
The sergeant returned his notepad to his pocket.

A few minutes later, the medical helicopter arrived and hovered over the port side of the deck. An Emergency Medical Technician wearing an orange jumpsuit dropped a trail line from the right side helicopter door. Foster held the line while Pavio kept the boat on course. One of the EMTs was traversing down to the yacht by a strop harness. He was tall, young, and well built.

As he knelt beside Jeff, he asked the sergeant, "What happened?"

"He hit the boat with a jet ski and has a slash on the forehead. I put a pressure dressing on it."

The EMT checked Jeff's vitals, "You did a good job on his dressing."

After stabilizing Jeff, the technician called for the litter. A litter was lowered from the helicopter, and the EMT and the sergeant placed Jeff in it. Jeff still had his flotation device on, but he still required the protective helmet before he could be hoisted on board the helicopter. He was strapped in, and the litter was hoisted up and taken inside the chopper.

"Where are you taking him?" the sergeant asked the EMT.

"Stony Brook University Hospital."

The helicopter hoisted the EMT up in the strop. Pavio moved the yacht toward the starboard side as the helicopter's engines roared and sped off with Jeff.

The investigation turned to Pavio. Sergeant Foster removed his hat for a second and scratched his head. He returned his cap to his head and took his notepad from his pocket once again and continued.

"Name, please?"

"Pavio Kravets."

"Can I see some identification?"

The boat pilot reached into his front pocket and pulled out his wallet. He slipped out his license and handed it to the sergeant. The sergeant wrote in his notebook: Pavio Kravets, 6400 Ocean Boulevard, Apartment 23B, Brighton Beach, New York.

"Let's get your statement," the sergeant ordered.

"I was traveling from Port Jefferson down Long Island Sound to the marina."

"What marina?"

"The Brooklyn Marina at Pier 5 in Brooklyn Bridge Park."

"How fast were you traveling?"

"About 20 knots."

"OK, how did the accident happen?"

"As I explained, I was traveling about 20 knots, and they were jumping my rear wakes. Then suddenly, they decided to pass me on my port side, and the jet ski just turned back and slammed into my side."

"Can I see the papers for the yacht?" Sergeant Foster continued the questioning.

Pavio went into a cabin drawer and pulled out the registration and insurance documents. He handed them to the sergeant.

"The papers say the yacht is registered to Lyresa Imports, Inc. What's your relation?"

"I'm employed by Lyresa Imports."

Just then the patrol boat returned. "Any luck?" asked the sergeant.

"No luck on the missing person, but I did locate the damaged jet ski in the weeds about half a mile from here. I notified dispatch to have it picked up," was the officer's response.

The sergeant turned toward Pavio, "We'll have to impound the yacht while we finish the investigation. Follow the police boat," he ordered. "I'll remain on board."

LEONARD DI GREGORIO

CHAPTER TWO

1:45 p.m. Suffolk County Police Station

Sergeant Foster entered the police station. "Morning Sarge, looks like your ass is trying desperately to stay in the chair but failing."

"Funny, I'm hysterical laughing," answered the desk sergeant.

" While you're at it, did you find Jeff Flynn's next of kin?"

"Still trying. I will let you know as soon as I can," answered the grey-haired sergeant, his glasses sliding off his nose.

"What's the status of the second victim?"

"Coast Guard has three choppers searching the sound, and we've notified the police departments along both Long Island and the Connecticut shorelines. Nothing yet," the desk sergeant continued, "By the way, Chief's in. He'll want to see your incident report."

"Figures. Soon as I write it up. Can you check this in for me?" said Foster tossing the property envelope on the desk.

"Sure, no problem."

Foster made his way to the backroom, found his metal desk that had seen better days, and turned on the computer. He settled his muscular 210 pounds into the seat, adjusted the chair to fit his 6-foot 3-inch frame, and removed his cap from his shaved head. A graduation photo from John Jay College of Criminal Justice was on his desk. The picture showed an original afro style hair under the cap. He completed the report and proceeded into the Chief's office, an office that screamed for a makeover or rehab as they would call it today, the last being in the late sixties. Police chiefs deserved an upgrade if you can call it one.

Chief Dale Thomas was sitting at his desk. Thomas was getting close to retirement, and his vanity had caused him to color his grey hair black. Everyone knew it was dyed, but he did keep himself in good shape. Foster turned in the report. After reading it, he looked up at the sergeant and asked what he thought.

"Doesn't sit right with me. This Pavio guy showed no emotion, but I had no other witnesses to question."

"OK, we'll hold it aside and wait for the victim's statement. If he doesn't make it, I'll turn it over to the detectives."

"Meanwhile, they located Flynn's parents. They live at 100 Oak Drive, Port Jeff. You want to take it, or should I call a sector car?"

"No. I'll do it," stated Foster, taking the slip from the Chief's desk as he left the office.

Foster slowly walked up the long walkway to the 3500 square foot house on the hill. It was a two-story, federal blue and trimmed white colonial with a wraparound porch. The house had been recently painted. The lawn looked freshly mowed. He walked up the four steps and knocked on the red door.

A well-dressed man in khaki slacks, a blue short-sleeved shirt, and boat shoes peered through the door and opened it.

He was in his sixties, a shade under six feet, grey crewcut hair, about 185 pounds.

"Can I help you?"

"Yes, I'm Sergeant Mike Foster of the Suffolk County Police. Do you have a son by the name of Jeff Flynn age 32, living at 60 Laurel?"

"Yes, what's wrong?" John Flynn asked, his tanned face turning pale.

"He's had an accident and is at Stony Brook University Hospital. He's in serious condition, but I don't know much more yet. If you'd like, I can take you there now."

"Yes, but I'd like to take my car. Can I follow you?"

"Sure."

"Thanks, please, let me get my wife. She's upstairs."

"OK, I'll be waiting in my car."

As the two cars departed, the sector car had its siren screeching, its red lights flashing. John Flynn followed close behind with his emergency flashers on.

Shortly after their arrival, at Stony Brook University Hospital, the sergeant took the Flynns directly to the emergency room.

He was stopped by a young woman in blue scrubs, "Can I help you?"

Mike Foster flashed his badge. He thought, *She has the most appealing strawberry blond hair.*

"I'm Sergeant Mike Foster. We're here to see Jeff Flynn. They brought him in earlier today," he said with a smile.

"Nice to meet you. I'm Danielle McGregor, the charge nurse for this floor," she looked down at her chart, " He's still in surgery."

"Any idea how long before he's out?"

Danielle tugged on Foster's arm, motioning him to move a few feet down the hall. "Can't tell. He was in bad shape when he arrived. They're doing everything they can."

Foster turned to Jeff's parents. "It might be hours before you can see him. Is there anything else I can do for you?"

"No. We'll stay here. We'd go crazy at home. Thanks, Sergeant Foster."

Foster handed Danielle McGregor his card. "I'd appreciate an update on Jeff. I want to speak to him as soon as possible."

"I'll do my best."

After hours of pacing, hand wringing, and the occasional updates from the hospital staff, the Flynns reluctantly returned home for a few hours of rest. They needed to recharge and contact Holly, their daughter.

CHAPTER THREE

10:00 a.m, Rhode Island School of Design

Holly Flynn stood in front of Jason Smith, Dean of Fine Arts at Rhode Island School of Design (RISD). The Dean was in his usual attire. He was wearing his bowtie with a checked blue and white button-down collared shirt. A blue herringbone wool blazer with arm patches, tan slacks, and brown shoes completed his outfit. They were in Smith's office on the third floor of the administration building. The corner office had a limited view overlooking the Providence River and Market Square Park. It was decorated in a scholarly motif with a wall of books and a grand redwood presidential desk atop an oriental carpet. The art deco chandelier gave the room a warm glow. There were still various modern art paintings on the walls to identify the Fine Arts department's present-day leadership in its field. A heart pine floor and fireplace screamed of the antiquity of this late 1800's brick building.

"Thank you for coming, Ms. Flynn. Please sit down."

"Good morning, Dean. You said you wanted to discuss something with me?" Holly asked.

"I just wanted to go over your plans for after graduation. It's been a while since we talked," said Dean Smith pushing his glasses back with his right index finger.

"Well, yes, that's true. I've been busy working on my thesis."

"Which is?" Jason responded.

"Leonardo da Vinci's Math; The relationship of Math in Art."

"Oh, yes. I remember now. Well, you graduated from Stoney Brook University Summa Cum Laude with a BA degree and then received a finance degree from Boston College, and now I believe you will leave us with your masters in fine arts, with distinction if your thesis is as good as the rest of your work."

"Thank you. I've put in a lot of time these past two years."

"Sometimes, we have to sacrifice to achieve our goals."

"Yes, but I do miss the outside relationships."

"You mean the dating scene?"

"Not exactly, but I had to leave someone to get this far in my life."

"It must have been difficult, but I'm sure it will work out."

"You never know. We're still close and speak frequently."

"Anyway, the reason I called for this meeting is I wanted to know what your plans are. Will you be going back to the love that you left and get married or move on to other goals?"

"Marriage is not in my future at this time. I want to achieve my career first."

"I understand money must come first. It gives independence."

"Oh no! You've got it wrong. I am independent financially, but I want to make it on my own and be able to say I was a success in the world."

"So, you are prepared to go out and make your mark."

"Exactly."

"Well, I just got off the phone with an old college friend. He's an art curator for a small but prestigious art museum in Boston."

"Which one?" Holly asked excitedly.

"Sorry, I am not at liberty to say as he will be leaving for another position after this summer. He has already given his notice, but the head of the establishment wants to hold off on the announcement until the summer. Meanwhile, he has the task of searching out his potential replacement."

"Great, but how would I qualify?"

"The thing is they are looking for someone smart, knowledgeable, and reliable."

"Again, why me?"

"You're intelligent, knowledgeable, and reliable. Your work at the Rusty Chicken gallery in Marblehead gives you some experience. But the bigger issue is you are at the beginning of your career and could grow into the position."

"That still doesn't work. What is the real reason you think I would be a perfect fit?"

"Sometimes, I think you are too smart," said a smiling Jason. "They can't afford to pay the appropriate salary commensurable with the position. But this would give you the prestige you are looking for."

"OK. You've got my interest."

"Great. I'll let you know more as soon as I can. I think this would be a great opportunity for you."

"Thank you, Dean Smith."

"Always a pleasure. Enjoy your day."

With renewed vigor, Holly left for the library to work on her thesis.

Holly was in the school library when her cell phone vibrated. She glanced at it and noticed the call was from home.

She left her books on the table and moved into the hallway.

"Hi, Mom. I've meant to call, but with working on my thesis, it's been crazy here."

"That's not why I called," her father corrected.

"Your brother's been in a horrible boating accident and is in critical condition here at Stony Brook Hospital. Your mother and I are waiting for him to get out of the operating room. She's frantic."

"Oh! My god. How'd it happen?"

"He was on his jet ski with another person, and they ran into a yacht. They were thrown overboard. He fractured his skull, and who knows what else."

"OK. I need to give the school some notice, and I'll drive down. I should be there sometime tonight."

"Thanks, but be careful. We have enough to worry about."

"Does Mom want to speak to me?"

"No. She's too upset right now, but she'll talk to you when you get here."

"Love you."

"Love you too."

Holly hung up and dialed the Art Department.

11:10 p.m.

Holly parked in front of the family home in Port Jefferson. The 5 foot 8 inch, green-eyed redhead, could have passed for a Manhattan model. Her wardrobe: a red turtleneck sweater, blue jeans, and calf-high tan boots, made her look ten years younger than her forty years. Holly stepped out of her metallic blue BMW.

She looked up with her light green eyes, at the home in which she grew up. A light breeze swept a strand of hair across her lips. She brushed it aside as she reminisced. Her green eyes glistened as she recalled her brother Jeff and the snowball fights during the long cold Long Island winters. Holly thought about all the times she pushed her little brother on the swing when he was a small child. *I pray Jeff's injuries are not as severe as my father said. Could the swing I pushed my baby brother on still be in the back yard. He's a man now. Time to put on the brave face and make the grand entrance. Not looking forward to this. Mom will probably give me that look like she's still waiting for the first grandchild.*

CHAPTER FOUR

100 Oak Drive, Port Jefferson

A somber John came to the door. He greeted Holly. They walked into the living room where Pat, her mother, sat on the sofa. Pat could barely hold back the tears, her hands folded across her lap, pearl rosary beads pressed between her fingers. Holly walked over and kissed her mother's cheek. Pat looked pale. She still had her petite young girl stature. Pat shared Holly's green eyes, but the red-dyed hair set them apart.

"Any word from the hospital?"

"He's out of the operating room but still in a coma. They told us the first forty-eight hours would be the most critical," a sniffling Pat responded.

"Pat, there's nothing to do until morning. Why don't you take a sleeping pill and go to bed? I'll get Holly settled in."

Pat kissed Holly on the cheek and went up to her bedroom for the night.

"Why don't you make us some coffee? I'll unpack and we can talk?" Holly suggested.

"Good idea."

A few minutes later, Holly returned. Both took seats at the kitchen table. John poured two cups of coffee and offered Holly the cream and sugar.

"No, thanks. I now drink it black. So tell me again. What happened?"

John fumbled with the spoon as he put the two teaspoons of sugar into his cup. He repeated all he learned from the police sergeant and the hospital nurse.

"Who was the other person on the jet ski?"

"They don't know, and he's still missing."

"Was Jeff driving or the other person?"

"The pilot of the boat stated he believes it was Jeff. It's Jeff's Jet Ski."

"Jeff has always been conscientious on that thing. He said he'd seen too many accidents. I find it hard to believe he would be driving recklessly, especially with another person on board."

"I agree, but who knows at this point? Hopefully, we'll learn some more when Jeff wakes."

"Let's hope. Till tomorrow." Holly kissed her father on the forehead and headed toward her bedroom. "Goodnight, Dad."

"Goodnight, sweetheart. Thanks for coming."

Monday at 9:00 a.m.

Mike entered the Suffolk precinct. He stopped at the coffee pot and poured himself a cup of black coffee, turned to the sugar bowl and added three scoops. His in-basket, atop his desk, contained a dozen case folders requiring his attention. He was interested in only one: yesterday's. Retrieving the folder from the pile, he noticed the statement from a night patrol officer detailing a truck matching the description located at the Port Jefferson Boat Launch at 9:35 p.m.

His chief called him into the office.

"They found the truck."

"So I see. Did they find anything else?"

"Just pulled into the impound yard. I'm in a bind. Two of my detectives were assigned to Nassau County. I need you to take this one."

"Sure, no problem. Can I wear my blue suit?"

"Yeah, take it out of mothballs," said the chief, smiling. "But first, why don't you go take a look at the truck?"

"Anything on the second victim?"

"Not yet. Coast Guard called off the search. Still waiting to hear from the shore precincts."

"Oh, by the way, good morning."

"Too early to say that," responded the chief.

Mike pulled into the impound yard and was directed to the pickup truck by the yard officer. He put on a pair of rubber gloves. Then he opened the glove compartment and went through the papers: a copy of the original window sale tag, registration, insurance card, and one black leather wallet with $120 and a library card with Jeff Flynn's name. The visors were clean. He checked between the seats, nothing. Behind the seats, nothing. Under the seats, a wallet. *Hallelujah.*

He opened the wallet. It read, Stepan Bondar, 22 Short Street, Lake Grove, NY.

Mike went back into the impound yard office and registered the items he found. He signed out the wallet and placed it in a clear plastic bag. He headed for Lake Grove.

12 Noon

Twenty-two Short Street was a small grey one-story ranch, with black shutters and one car attached garage. There were two boys' bikes in the driveway. He rang the doorbell. A blond woman opened the door with long braided hair. She was tall, taller than him, not thin but not fat, well-built as they say. In her late twenties or early thirties, he guessed.

"Mrs. Bondar?" Mike displayed his badge.

"Yes?"

"Is your husband at home?"

"No, not at the moment."

"Do you know where he is?"

"He went boating with his friend, Jeff, yesterday. It's a ritual of his." She shrugged her shoulders with a sign of indifference. "They usually drink too much. He stays overnight. Why! Is something wrong?"

"I'm sorry, there's been an accident, and your husband is missing," explained Mike.

A quivering Anna Bondar questioned the sergeant. "That can't be. He's on a boating trip."

"It was a boating accident. Jeff Flynn is in the hospital unconscious, and Stepan is missing."

"Please come in." Anna slowly walked into the living room and sat on the sofa. She tried holding back the tears. But she couldn't hold them back for long. "When did it happen?"

"Yesterday at approximately 10 A.M. It's been over twenty-four hours since the Coast Guard began their search of the sound. We've contacted all the precincts along both shores, but we've heard nothing yet."

"What'll I do? What do I tell my boys?" a hysterical Anna pleaded.

"Do you have any relatives close by?"

"In Brighton Beach. I guess I can call someone."

"That would be a good idea."

"Before I leave, can I ask you a few questions?"

"If it will help find Stepan."

"Thank you. I'll be brief."

"What was he wearing?"

"I think he had on a red t-shirt with some fish on the front, blue shorts, and black sneakers."

"Do you have a recent picture of Stepan?"

"Oh, yes. Of course. Here's a recent picture," she handed the sergeant a photo from atop the mantle.

"Thanks, I'll let you know as soon as we have something."

Mike Foster reached for the doorknob and turned. "Oh, one more thing. Did they go out the night before?"

"No, he was home all night."

Mike returned to his car and called into the precinct. The desk sergeant answered, and Foster gave him the description of Stepan Bondar. Next call, Stony Brook University Hospital.

"Nurses' station," curtly answered a frazzled Danielle McGregor.

"This is Sergeant Foster. I need the status of Jeff Flynn. He was admitted yesterday."

"Oh, yes, Mike, I didn't forget you, but he's still heavily sedated."

"Is he in a coma?"

"No, but during the few moments he was awake he was confused. I don't believe he will give you any reliable information yet."

"Thanks, I'll call back."

He disconnected the call and decided to stop at Panera Bread to pick up some lunch.

Back at the precinct, he laid his Panera bag containing black coffee with sugar, a chicken panini, and a small tomato bisque soup on his desk.

Lunch was interrupted by the desk sergeant. "Just heard they located the second victim in Stony Brook. He's on the way to the morgue."

"Thanks, I'll take a trip later," he continued, as he finished his lunch. *It looks like I have a corpse on my hands.*

Monday 2:00 p.m., Twenty-two Short Street

Mike knocked on the door.

"Can I help you?" sharply asked the muscular man standing well over six feet tall, blocking the door. His black hair was hanging down to his shoulders. There were *blackwork* tattoos[1] on his neck and forearms protruded from under his black jogging suit. He had a four-inch scar on the right side of his face.

"I'm looking for Mrs. Bondar. I have information about her husband."

---

[1] Black ink in various geometric designs

"She lying down. I get her," replied Alexi Danko in his broken English with a strong Russian accent.

A moment later, a red-eyed Anna came out of the bedroom.

"We believe we have located Stepan."

"Is he all right?"

"I'm sorry to say; he's not."

"Is he alive?" asked Anna.

"No."

Anna rushed into her bedroom.

"I need someone to identify him."

"I'll go," announced Alexi, "Give me a minute to calm Anna."

A few minutes later, he returned and followed the sergeant to the car.

The sign on the building at 725 Veterans Memorial Highway in Hauppauge read *Suffolk County Medical Examiner.* Sergeant Foster parked in a reserved parking spot next to the building. They passed through security, and the officer directed them to the elevator down the hall. The morgue was in the basement. The ME greeted them as they walked in. A covered body was lying on a stainless steel gurney. The ME pulled back the sheet covering the body. Alexi's face went pale. He fought back the tears, "Yes, that is Stepan."

They proceeded to the ME's desk, signed the identification papers and left.

"Can I have the funeral parlor pick him up?"

"Not yet. We may have to perform an autopsy first to confirm the cause of death."

"I understand, but we are Jewish and require a quick burial. Usually, within twenty-four hours."

"Understood. The ME, who is also Jewish, assured me he would complete the examination as soon as possible. We will call you as soon as the COD is available."

"What?" Alexi asked with a confused look.

"Sorry, Cause of Death," answered Mike.

They returned to the car for the trip back to Lake Grove.

"How well do you know Stepan?" Mike asked nonchalantly.

"I'm Anna's cousin, but I work with Stepan at JFK Airport. Excuse me; worked with Stepan. We came here from Russia together about twelve years ago."

"Who do you work for at JFK?"

"I work at Ground Services of America (GSA). It is an airfreight handling company."

"Wow, it must be exciting. I always wanted to work at the airport."

"Not as exciting as you think. We both worked in the cargo area for a handling company, not directly for an airline. We don't get all the benefits you hear about. Those are only for airline personnel."

"Oh, too bad."

Mike pulled up to 22 Short Street, and Alexi left the car.

"If I have any other questions, I'll call you. I'd rather not bother Anna at this time if I can help it."

"Sure," Alexi handed Foster a GSA card with his cell number written on the back.

Tuesday 8:00 a.m.

The M.E.'s report was on top of Sergeant Foster's desk. It read, "cause of death due to multiple lacerations of the torso and asphyxiation by drowning."

Mike decided to call the hospital. He asked to speak to Nurse McGregor, but she was unavailable. The nurse took his message to have her call him back.

He was still going over the report when his phone rang.

"Good morning Mike, this is Danielle McGregor at Stony Brook Hospital. I'm sorry I couldn't take your call, but I was with a patient."

"I understand."

"Jeff's still not able to respond to questions."

"I'm sorry for the interruptions, but I need to talk to him as soon as possible."

"I understand."

"OK, thanks, Danielle. Please keep me informed if anything changes."

"Of course, Mike," answered Danielle.

Mike proceeded into the Chief's office to update him on the case.

Chief Thomas was on the phone and waved his hand towards the chair opposite his desk. Mike Foster took the cue and sat down.

When the call ended, Thomas turned to Mike, "That was the DA. She wants to know what we are doing with this case."

"I still have not been able to question the only other witness, Jeff Flynn. The only statement from the boat pilot, Pavio, states Jeff Flynn ran into the yacht."

"I'll call the DA back to see if she wants to proceed with a homicide case against Jeff Flynn."

"Why, homicide? I thought I was investigating a boating accident."

"Seems they found traces of alcohol in Flynn's blood. The DA's looking at charging this guy with criminal negligence."

"What's she running for office?" Mike asked with a surprised look on his face.

"Something like that," mumbled the Chief as Mike got up to leave.

CHAPTER FIVE

New York Daily News, September 22, 2017. Obituary Section

*S*tepan Bondar. September 19, 2017, of Lake Grove, NY. Cherished husband of Anna Bondar. Beloved father of Borys Bondar and Leonid Bondar. Relatives and friends are invited to services Thursday, September 23, at 11:00 a.m. at Kehila Chapels Inc., 60 Brighton, and 11th St. Brooklyn, NY. The family will return to the residence of Mr. & Mrs. Mykhailo Chernov for Shiva.

Wednesday 6:00 p.m.

The Flynn family was conducting their bedside ritual at Stony Brook Hospital. Jeff was still in a coma. The attending physician, Dr. Richardson, had just updated the family with some positive news that Jeff's head injuries were improving.

"I think it's a good sign. Don't you?" Pat asked John. Her face was trying to smile.

"Yes, dear, I do, and the doctors plan on waking him tomorrow afternoon."

"There's nothing you can do here. Why don't we go back to the house?" Holly suggested.

They all agreed.

Back at the house, Holly brought in the newspapers that had piled up on the stoop for the past couple of days. She read the obituary section and noticed one for Stepan Bondar.

"Do you mind going to the hospital alone tomorrow?" Holly asked.

"Of course not. Why?" answered John.

"I noticed they have something for Stepan at 11 a.m. I think it would be a good idea if one of us attended."

"If you like. Sure. He was Jeff's friend."

Thursday 11:00 a.m.

Holly waited in her car for the last of the people to enter the Kehila Chapel. It was a large group of friends and family.

Stepan was popular and loved by his friends and neighbors. Finally, she entered. She noticed all the women's heads were covered. Fortunately, she had a black scarf in her bag. She placed it on her head. Skullcaps (Kippahs) were in a basket at the entrance for the men. She found the last seat in the last row. She took it. The ceremony started. It was strange to Holly. It was her first time in a Jewish chapel. A stranger next to her smiled and nodded his head.

He was a bit over six feet tall with a muscular build and black, short curly hair. The small crow's feet by the sides of his eyes and the lines across his forehead revealed his forty-plus years of age.

The Rabbi said some prayers and then announced that a couple of Stepan's friends would like to say something.

"Thank you, Rabbi. I will be short. I am Mykhailo Chernov. Stepan worked for me since he first came to this country. He always made me laugh with his jokes. Stepan never could remember the...how you say, punch line. He called me Uncle Mike. I called him son."

Holly listened intently.

One more followed.

"Most of you know me. I am Alexi Danko. Stepan and I came here from Russia together. He married my cousin, Anna, and started a family. We were brothers, always together. I will miss him," said Alexi, unable to hold back the tears.

Holly noticed the black tattoos on Alexi's neck and arms. A chill passed through her body.

In the end, the pallbearers carried out the coffin, and people took turns walking alongside him as he moved to the hearse.

Holly exited the chapel. On her way to her car, the stranger who had smiled at her started walking towards her.

"Hi, I couldn't help but notice you felt out of place. You're not Jewish, are you?"

"No, Irish."

"How did you know, Stepan?"

"He was my brother's friend. But, he's in the hospital and couldn't come."

"Your bother was the other man on the jet ski?"

"Yes."

"I'm sorry, how is he?"

"He's still in the hospital. They hope to see some improvement later this afternoon."

"Are you going to the cemetery?"

"I didn't plan to. Where is it?"

"Beth Moses in Farmingdale. I could go with you if you like? I want to talk to you about what happened if it's OK?"

"I'd like that, but how will you get back?"

"Oh, I'll catch a ride with one of the others."

"I'm Holly Flynn," said Holly as she offered her hand.

"Moshe Kaplan, glad to meet you." Moshe accepted Holly's handshake with a smile.

During the ride to the cemetery, Moshe explained that he had worked with Stepan for the past year at JFK Airport. He stated that they had a close friendship for the last two months. Holly wondered if Stepan could have pushed her brother into doing something foolish. She asked Moshe what kind of man was Stepan?

"Oh, Stepan was a great guy. Loved his wife and children above all else, and he loved the United States. Thought this was the greatest country ever."

"Was he reckless?"

"Never. Stepan loved his family too much to take foolish chances. Why do you ask?"

"Because my brother wasn't reckless, either. I can't believe they would be that close to the front of that boat to crash into it."

"Neither can I."

Just then, they arrived at the cemetery. Holly and Moshe exited the car and joined the procession to the gravesite. At the end of the ceremony, the family picked up a shovel from a pile of dirt. Each member dropped a shovelful onto the casket. After returning the shovel to the dirt pile, and another member repeated the ritual. Finally, the mourners passed by the family.

Holly was about to approach Anna and pay her respects, but Moshe advised against it.

"This is not done until shiva at home later."

"I didn't know that. Please give Anna my condolences."

"Of course."

"Thank you."

As they walked back to the car, Moshe explained to Holly how to get back to Port Jefferson as he would be leaving with one of the other mourners.

"Moshe, I would like to talk to you some more about Stepan. Do you think you can find some time to join me in a cup of coffee or something? I would be willing to meet you wherever you chose."

"I'd also like to talk some more. I'll get back to you tomorrow."

"Great, here, let me give you my cell number," she said as she pulled out a pad from her purse. She handed the paper to Moshe, "Thanks for keeping me company on this long trip."

"My pleasure. I'll call you tomorrow." Moshe waved goodbye.

As she approached her car, she spotted Alexi staring at her. She started to perspire. The same chill passed through her body once again. Quickly, she entered her car, locked the doors, and left for the hospital.

CHAPTER SIX

Moscow, winter, years earlier…

Ten year old Stepan Bondar left school after his last class. Overcast skies blocked the sunlight. It was a typical winter in Moscow, bitter cold and snowing steadily. Two teenage boys were waiting for him. They were Chechen sympathizers. Russians had reportedly killed 267 civilians in the raid on Gudermes just months ago. The Chechen war had been going on for the last three years. Many Russians were against it. As Stepan walked by, one of the boys pushed his books out of his hands. The books fell onto the snow-covered pavement. The school books scattered in the snow. As he bent over to pick up the books, a second boy kicked him in his rear end. He went down, his face now in the snow. The boy then kneeled on top of him. "Get off me," he tried to yell but his mouth spits out snow. They were laughing at him. The boy finally got off him. Stepan tried to stand but he slipped on the ice that had formed under the snow. Once again, he was punched in the face by one of the thugs. The bitter cold just added to his pain. When he was eventually able to get his footing, he took a swing at one of his assailants. He missed. They started kicking him, and he fell on the ground. He was in excruciating pain.

Suddenly, another boy appeared. He grabbed one of Stepan's attackers and threw him to the ground. The other thug took a swipe at the stranger. The stranger caught his hand and pulled it high across the boys back until he heard a crack. The teenager cried in pain. The second boy pulled a knife and slashed the stranger on the side of his face. A kick to the groin and the teenager dropped the knife. The assailants took off running. Stepan looked up at the extended hand from the stranger and took it. He helped him up.

"What's your name, comrade?"

"Stepan, Stepan Bondar," answered Stepan, still shaking.

"Alexi Danko, I think you need an older brother. I will be him."

"You are bleeding," noticed Stepan.

"Just a small cut," answered Alexi.

Alexi looked over Stepan. "I see no blood on you, but your face is very red."

"It was in the snow a great part of the time."

Alexi laughed, and finally, so did Stepan.

After Stepan picked up the books, they walked home together.

Years later, they were walking down the street. A truck was making deliveries to a clothing store. The truck stopped and parked. The driver pulled open the back door, and there were racks of men's long coats to be delivered to the store nearby. With an arm full of coats, the driver entered the store.

Alexi looked both ways and jumped onto the truck. He looked at Stepan and called out.

"What size are you?"

"Medium, why?"

Three medium coats came flying out of the truck. Alexi jumped down with another six.

"Run!" he yelled.

After running for five blocks, they finally stopped. Stepan was trying to catch his breath.

"I'm exhausted. What have we done?" questioned an astonished Stepan.

"We got coats for the winter," answered a smiling Alexi.

"That's stealing."

"No, we give them back next spring," chuckled Alexi, then continued, "You know, we should go to U.S.A. I hear everything free there. I have uncle. He help us."

"I would like that."

"Someday, little brother, we go to U.S.A."

Sheremetyevo International Airport, Moscow, Russia, Friday, June 16, 2006

Alexi Danko and Stepan Bondar had arrived three hours early for their 9:20 a.m. flight from Sheremetyevo International Airport in Moscow. There was plenty of time to wait before boarding their Aeroflot flight to JFK International Airport in Jamaica, New York. The airport passenger terminal seemed huge to Stepan. This being his first time on a plane or for that matter the first time in an airport, he was extremely fidgety. Even though this was also Alexi's first time, he played the big brother role and took charge.

Stepan looked at Alexi, "We are finally on our way to the United States."

"Yes," answered Alexi, "just like we swore we would for the last ten years."

"What did your uncle say when you told him we were coming."

"He said, 'I have jobs for you. You will start work on Monday'."

"That's only three days after we arrive." Stepan continued, "Will we have enough time to find an apartment?"

"Don't worry, my uncle Mykhailo explained, 'It is all arranged.' He has an apartment for us in Brighton Beach. It has a large Russian Jewish population. I have relatives there."

The walk to their departure gate took some time, and as they strolled through the terminal, they were amazed at the number of stores and restaurants. It was the biggest mall they had ever seen. It had more shops than most small towns in Russia. As the terminal was relatively empty this early in the morning, the announcements over the loudspeakers caused an echo. As they passed the duty-free shop, Stepan stopped short.

"Alexi, we must stop here and get a gift for your Uncle Mykhailo."

They walked into the duty-free shop surrounded by French perfumes, American cigarettes, Cuban cigars, and liquors from around the world.

"What should we get him?" Stepan continued, "Perhaps, some cigarettes."

"No! We get him some Cuban cigars, I don't think he can get them in America," answered Alexi.

"Good, then I will get him some good Russian Vodka. A taste of home from mother Russia."

They picked up their packages and proceeded to their departure gate. Moments later, they had boarded and strapped into their seats at the rear of the aircraft. Members of the cabin crew took positions in the aisles and gave their safety presentations. Stepan took in every word and read the small instruction pamphlet that was in his seat pocket. Would he need a life preserver if they crashed? He looked under his seat to be sure it was there. The aircraft left the gate and took its position on the runway. The captain pushed the throttles forward, and the colossal plane roared down the runway, engines screaming. As the aircraft traveled down the long runway its speed increased and finally left the ground. The thrust of the speeding aircraft pushed Alexi and Stepan back in their seats. Stepan squeezed the armrest tightly. With the nose heading for the clouds, Stepan saw his city of Moscow shrinking and finally disappearing under the clouds. He jerked in his seat as the pilot pulled up the landing wheels and locked them into place. Eventually, they leveled off, and the flight attendant offered them a drink. The remainder of the flight went without incident, and Stepan finally became more comfortable flying for the first time.

JFK International Airport Arrivals Building

It was 12:05 p.m. when they finally arrived in New York. The ten-hour flight was exhausting, and even though it was only noon in New York, it was still ten p.m. to Stepan and Alexi. After they disembarked the aircraft, they had to follow the crowd through the terminal hallway into the US Immigration area. Some wide-body aircraft, carrying hundreds of passengers each, seemingly arrived at the same time. Masses of people from around the world, all coming to New York, had formed lines waiting to be interviewed and passed into America. All Stepan could think of was where they could fit all these people in New York. Hours passed before they had completed the arrival process and sorted out their luggage. As they walked out into the terminal, there was a receiving line of what looked like over a hundred people looking for their relatives and friends. There holding a large sign stating, "Welcome Alexi," was a smiling Mykhailo.

An hour later, they entered a two-bedroom, two-bath condo in Brighton Beach, Brooklyn. The apartment was modestly furnished. There was a small galley kitchen with a dining area outside. A living room area included a sofa, two lounge chairs, and a coffee table. The twenty-one-inch color television completed the room. Nothing elaborate, but it would do for the time being for the two bachelors.

Since the refrigerator was bare, Mykhailo took them food shopping at a nearby supermarket. Stepan was amazed at the variety of food. He had never had as many choices in Russia. Mykhailo and Stepan paid the bill, and Alexi rolled the cart to the car. After storing everything in the apartment, Mykhailo said he would pick them up on Monday at seven a.m. He handed them each fifty dollars in US currency. After Mykhailo left, they slept until the next day. Sunday, they explored their new neighborhood. They found many fellow Russians who had recently moved to the US.

Monday morning, Mykhailo picked them up and drove them for their first day at work. At GSA, they trained in forklift driving, loading and unloading cargo, proper documentation procedures, and eventually acceptance and handling of dangerous goods. After a few months, they got friendly with the rest of the workers and settled into life in America.

JFK International Airport, GSA Warehouse, July 2006

"Here, take this and put it in your car," said Alexi, handing a box to Stepan, "and don't let anyone see you do it."

"What is it?" Stepan asked.

"It's an Apple MacBook notebook computer. Just came out last month."

"Whose?"

"Yours. Now stop asking questions, little brother."

"But, I can't afford this," said Stepan flailing his hands above his head.

"It's free. A gift from Uncle Mykhailo. Now put it in the car."

"OK," said Stepan. He put the laptop in the trunk of his car.

That night Stepan asked Alexi, "What is going on? How come I got a MacBook?"

"Don't be such a putz. Where you think it come from? It fall off truck, OK!" Alexi's chin went forward, and he pointed a finger at Stepan's chest, "You know things are going on here that you should not question. You get paid, yes?"

"Yes," Stepan whispered.

"I don't hear you."

"YES!" Stepan shouted.

"You need to relax, Stepan. I think I will introduce you to my cousin."

The following week, Alexi arranged a double date for himself and Stepan.

They met at a nearby movie theater. Stepan arrived, and Alexi was already there, with his cousin Anna and her friend.

"Stepan, I would like you to meet my cousin, Anna Danko. Anna, meet my best friend, Stepan Bondar."

"So, glad to meet you," said the shy young girl in a Russian accent.

Stepan was mesmerized by her beautiful face and her long blond hair.

The date went well, but Stepan was too shy to ask Anna out again, so he asked Alexi to set up another double date. Alexi agreed, as did Anna. They double-dated for three nights in a row.

The following night Alexi suggested they once again double date, but Anna refused.

"Alexi, if Stepan wants to go out with me, he must ask me himself," she demanded.

That night Stepan got the courage to call Anna and ask for a date. She insisted that he pick her up at her house and meets her father, Kostas, and her mother, Leena. He agreed to pick her up at seven the next night.

Before this critical date, Stepan stopped at the barber and got a shave and haircut. He bought a new suit and shoes. For the first time in his life, Stepan had to meet a girl's parents, and he did not want to blow his chance on this one. He would arrive, looking at his best.

Alexi suggested Stepan bring a gift for Anna's mother and father. He suggested flowers or chocolates for her mother and cigars or vodka for her father.

Stepan decided on a bouquet of roses for Leena Danko but could not decide on the gift for Kostas. He asked Alexi for a recommendation.

"I would choose the vodka," answered Alexi.

"But what kind? I want to impress Kostas."

"Kauffman Collection Vodka. It is one of the hardest to get. Very expensive."

"But Alexi, how much is it?"

"Four hundred dollars. But I have a bottle from Uncle Mykhailo that I will give you."

"Alexi. I don't have that much money to spend on vodka."

"No problem, it is a gift. You will be family soon, I think."

Stepan accepted the offer, and roses and vodka would be the gifts.

Anna greeted Stepan at the door and took him into the living room. There sat her mother and father. Both had a stern look on their faces.

"Mother, this is Stepan," said Anna bringing him closer to her mother.

"I am glad to meet you, Mrs. Danko."

She nodded her head in acknowledgment but said nothing.

Stepan handed Leena the roses. She smiled.

Anna then took Stepan to meet her father.

As Stepan approached, Anna's father stood up. He was much taller than Stepan.

Stepan was shaking. The room was silent for what Stepan thought was hours, but was in reality, only minutes. Finally, her father looked at Stepan and put out his hand.

They shook hands, and Stepan was eventually able to say, "So glad to meet you, Mr. Danko."

Anna's father answered in Russian, "It is nice to meet one of Anna's friends."

Stepan handed Kostas the bottle of vodka.

Kostas grinned. He left the room and returned without the bottle.

The father continued the conversation asking Stepan where he came from in Russia. Kostas continued the questioning asking where Stepan went to school and what he was going to do with his life.

It didn't take long for Stepan to assure Mr. Danko that he was a stable person and respected in the community where he lived.

Mrs. Danko brought out the bottle of Kaufman vodka from the freezer and offered Stepan a drink.

That was just the beginning. Next, Mrs. Danko brought out some homemade food and insisted Stepan try everything.

They never went out on their planned date that night. Stepan finally left after midnight.

The following night was not much better, but he was able to take her out for dinner and dancing afterward. It seemed this ritual would go on forever as it did for the next month. Stepan realized he could not continue in this fashion and had to make a decision. When they arrived back at her house on their last date, he asked Anna to marry him. She said she would think it over.

One year later, they were married.

GSA Warehouse, October 2012, 6:00 a.m.
Alexi and Stepan arrived for the first shift. The management team was having their morning briefing in the second-floor offices.

They walked up to the time clock outside the supervisor's office and swiped their employee cards.

"Hey guys, come in here for a minute," yelled Frank Hanson, the shift supervisor.

"Hello, Frank, what's up," asked Alexi.

"I need an inventory check," said Frank, handing Alexi the print out of the day's inventory.

"No problem," Alexi took the sheets. "Do you have a clipboard?"

"Sure." Frank opened his desk drawer and handed one to Stepan.

After they walked out into the warehouse, Alexi and Stepan began to check each warehouse location and confirmed each shipment was in the proper aisle. The process took just under an hour to complete. Everything was in order except for one delivery. Two boxes of perfume were missing from location B12. Stepan remembered placing them in the location yesterday. He checked the paperwork and found it was still not released from Customs.

They reported back to Frank, and he jotted something on his notepad.

"I believe it is stolen. I unloaded it myself," advised Stepan.

"Thanks, I'll call our claims department and report it missing. You guys go out and take care of the customers. There's a backlog of truckers in the docks."

Stepan and Alexi left Frank's office.

"Isn't he going to call the police?" asked Stepan.

"You heard him. Let him handle it. It's none of our business."

"But…"

"No, buts, just do your job," advised Alexi.

They strolled up to the front counter and pulled the next pickup orders.

"Franco trucking?" yelled out, Stepan.

"Here. I'm in bay number nine," answered one of the seated truckers.

Stepan jumped on a forklift and pulled the shipment of ten cartons of shoes located in B6. As he approached door nine, the driver was waiting. Stepan opened the overhead dock door, and the back of the vehicle was visible. There were two boxes of perfume sitting in the nose of the truck.

"Don't say anything," advised Alexi from his seat on the forklift in the next dock door.

After Stepan completed the loading and had the trucker sign off for the shipment, he turned to Alexi, "What's going on?"

"Look, things are going on that you should not get involved with."

"Why don't we call the police?"

"Because this was a special shipment meant for a certain customer. It must not have a paper trail to him."

"What about perfume? Won't the importer be upset?"

"The importer's insurance will pay, including a profit. He will be happy. The perfume was not worth that much anyway."

"Then why did he order it?"

"It was prearranged. The customer was never going to pick it up."

"I still do not understand," Stepan repeated.

"OK! The shipment was narcotics, not perfume. Do you want to have that little house on Long Island for your family? Uncle Mykhailo said he would loan you the money for the down payment. You will not make this kind of money on the outside. Anna, your beautiful wife, and two young boys need their father. Don't be stupid. Just shut your mouth and do your job."

Nothing more was said. Stepan went back to work. Two years later, Stepan and Anna moved into a small ranch with their sons, Michael and Alex.

CHAPTER SEVEN

Thursday 3 a.m., Stony Brook Hospital, present day...

D anielle McGregor greeted Holly outside the I.C.U with news that her brother was awake, and they believed he would pull through. She was allowed to see him, Danielle told Holly, but he was still disoriented and may not recognize everyone.

"Don't be surprised if Jeff thinks we're trying to kill him. He's going to say some strange things," offered Danielle.

"Got it. You're not a murderer," Holly answered, smiling.

Holly opened the door and entered the I.C.U. Pat and John were at Jeff's bed. His head wrapped in a turban of bandages. Tubes extended from his arms and nose. *I don't recognize this alien from another planet,* thought Holly. She kissed her mother on her cheek and Jeff on his forehead. She turned.

"How's he doing?"

"Jeff goes in and out. But at least he's partially awake. Can't make out what he's talking about."

"I know," Holly continued, "he's confused. Hopefully, he'll be better tomorrow."

"How was the service?" inquired John.

"Very nice. Very different. For a funeral, it went well, and I offered our condolences to Stepan's wife. I met a friend of Stepan's at the chapel, who rode with me to the cemetery. I found him interesting. He also doesn't understand how they could have crashed into the boat. I'm beat; it's been a long day. Are you guys staying?"

"No, I think he needs some rest. We'll come back tomorrow," sighed Pat.

They left.

Thursday, 4:00 p.m., Suffolk County DA's Office

Suffolk County District Attorney, Susan Shepard, was having a conference with two of her Assistant DA's, Michael Bibb and Richard Cavanaugh. The tall, slender brunette was wearing a navy blue pantsuit. A pink blouse whose opened collar laid over her jacket lapels gave Susan a relaxed yet business-like appearance. Her long hair draped down past her shoulders. They were meeting in a small conference room with a round oak table. Susan sat at the head of the table with Michael sitting on her right and Richard to her left. Both Assistant DA's were wearing similar black suits, white dress shirts, and red striped ties. There was one ample light shining over the table focusing on the folders that Susan had laid out before them. A TV monitor was hanging from one wall. A coffee urn sat on a small bookcase in the corner, but no one was drinking coffee. Light grey walls and a blue carpet completed the windowless room.

"I received a report this morning from Chief Dale Thomas over in Port Jefferson. An accident involving two males on a jet ski collided with a yacht killing one of the passengers. The owner of the watercraft is in Stony Brook Hospital with severe head injuries. According to the report, in front of you, the pilot of the yacht states that they were riding his wakes and looked like they were trying to pass when they made a sharp turn and ran into his boat. A report from the hospital shows both the driver and the deceased had a small amount of alcohol in their blood."

Michael interceded, "Why do we have this on the agenda?"

"For one thing, the area where the jet ski struck the yacht is forward of where the boat wake would propel them. The forward wake would not be strong enough to cause the jet ski to veer off course. It doesn't fit, and we can't interview the driver of the jet ski because he's in a coma."

"It looks like the best we can hope for is criminally negligent homicide," Richard offered.

"I agree," Michael stated.

"OK, let's set up an arraignment date pending Flynn's release from the hospital. Meanwhile, we can continue our investigation," said Susan. "Richard, can you arrange for an officer to be positioned at the hospital until then?"

"Yes."

"Before we leave, are there any other questions?" she asked.

Michael and Richard scanned through the folder. They both shook their heads.

"Good, let's do it. Have a great day."

Friday, Noon, Stony Brook Hospital

Once more, there was the ritual at Jeff's bedside.

"Do you know where you are?" asked Holly.

"Yes," Jeff responded.

"Where?"

"Home," answered Jeff.

"No, Jeff. You're in a hospital. You had a boating accident."

"Oh."

"What day is it?"

"Monday?"

"No, it's Friday."

"Who is he?" Holly pointed to one of the doctors.

"He's the head of the prison."

"No, Jeff. He's your doctor."

"Oh. He's my doctor." Jeff responded.

"Jeff, who am I?"

"Who are you?"

"Holly, I'm your sister, Holly."

"Oh, yeah, Holly."

"Who's that?"

"Dad?"

"Yes, good, that's dad, and that's mom over there."

"Look, that's the woman who tried to knife me last night," Jeff whispered, pointing to the nurse who was checking his vitals.

"Still having fun, Jeff?" the nurse asked.

"He should start remembering things tomorrow. We've reduced his medication, so he should begin to improve rapidly from now on.

Just keep asking him questions he should know," continued the nurse.

"We will. Thanks."

Just then, Holly's cell vibrated. She stepped outside the room.

Outside, she checked her voicemail. Moshe.

"I'm off tomorrow. Let's have lunch. Call me back."

Next, Holly called Moshe back.

"Holly, I'm so glad you called. Are you available for lunch tomorrow?"

"Sure. What time?"

"How's noon sound?"

"I think one would be better. The business lunch crowd will be finished, and it'll be less crowded."

"You're right. Let's make it after one p.m." Moshe continued, "Where would you like to go?"

"How much time do you have?"

"The whole day. So it's up to you."

Holly looked up at the sky. It was cloudless. She imagined a scene from her past having dinner at a restaurant by a bay in Massachusetts.

"Would you mind driving out to the island?" Holly asked.

"Of course not. Why? Where were you thinking?"

"There's a little restaurant in Centerport called the Mill Pond House. It's on the water, and although I haven't been there, I've only heard good things. I've always wanted to try it but just never got around to doing it."

"Sounds good. I'll meet you there."

"Great, see you then. Bye."

Now that lunch had been arranged with Moshe, perhaps she would get some questions answered. Holly decided she needed some fresh air to get her thoughts together. She left the building and found a quiet park across from the hospital. A bench was available for her to sit and meditate for a few moments. *The trees are turning colors, the air is crisp and clean, with a cloudless blue sky. It is fall. What to do next, perhaps this meeting with Moshe will help. He seems to be interested and interesting.*

Holly rose from the bench after thirty minutes past and returned to her brother's bedside.

"Holly, where've you been?" inquired an agitated John.

"I had a phone call. Why what's wrong?"

"We just found out they want to charge Jeff with criminally negligent homicide."

"For what?"

"They believe he was drunk when he crashed into the boat."

"That's crazy. You stay here. Let me make some calls. I'll see you at the house later."

"OK."

Holly sat in her car. *I need to talk to somebody who's not family.* She picked up her cell.

"Gallery 21."

"Cas, it's Holly."

"Hi Holly, How've you been?" answered Castle Rock, Holly's past lover, one-time boss, and owner of Gallery 21, a high-end art gallery in downtown Boston. Their relationship had ended amicably, and they still kept in touch frequently.

"Not good. My brother Jeff had a horrific boating accident. He's in I.C.U. at Stony Brook Hospital."

"Sorry to hear. How can I help?"

"They're charging him with criminally negligent homicide. I'm going to need a good lawyer."

"No problem, one of my customers at the gallery is the top defense lawyer here in Boston. I'll give him a call."

"Thanks. I owe you."

"Of course you do. It's been too long. Let me get on this and call you back."

"Thanks"

Holly hung up. She pulled a notebook from her handbag and started writing;

Need lawyer.

Need the police report.

Did they take a blood test at the hospital?

I need to know more about Stepan and the boat pilot.

Holly stopped at a diner and took a seat at a corner booth.

The waitress approached and asked, "Do you need a menu?"

"No, just coffee, please."

"Right away," she answered as she grabbed a set up from a nearby table and placed it in front of Holly.

As Holly waited, her leg began to shake. She placed the palm of her hand on her knee to stop it. Every muscle in her body was tight. It wasn't long before her eye twitched. *Get hold of yourself,* she thought. There would be no smile on her face today. Her lips drew tightly together. The wrinkles in her forehead did not help her disposition. She began to take deep long breaths, followed by closing her eyes and rolling her head. As her shoulders dropped, her body finally relaxed. It took a few moments for her nerves to calm down. When they did, she thought, *Moshe knew something.*

The coffee arrived, and she took that first sip and sighed. The cell phone in her purse rang.

"Holly, it's Cas, I have a contact in New York. His name is Samuel Baum of Baum and Belkin. They're located on Park Avenue in Manhattan. He knows you're calling."

"Do you have the number?"

"Oh! Yes. Here it is, 212-555-0150."

She put it in her cell. "Thanks, Cas, I'll call him now."

She tried to call, but her hand was shaking too much. After two tries, she got it right, and it went through.

"Baum and Belkin, how may I direct your call?" answered the receptionist.

"Mr. Samuel Baum, please."

"What is this about?" continued the receptionist.

"This is Holly Flynn. He was recommended to me by Castle Rock in Boston."

"Oh yes, Miss Flynn, he's expecting your call. I'll put you right through."

"Samuel Baum, how can I help you?"

"Hello, this is Holly Flynn."

"Hello, Holly. I've been waiting for your call. My colleague in Boston has requested me to handle the case personally. I plan on putting my best team on it. He told it was a criminally negligent homicide case, but not much else. What can you tell me?"

Holly explained what had transpired so far.

"I don't see much of a problem if what you told me so far is correct. We do require a $50,000.00 retainer before we start. Would that be a problem?"

"No. I'll wire you the retainer today."

"OK, we'll start on it immediately. I should have something within three days. Meanwhile, I suggest we keep Jeff in the hospital as long as possible and away from the police."

"There's a police officer stationed outside his room."

"I understand, but he is not to talk to the police without counsel at any time. Agreed?"

"Agreed."

CHAPTER EIGHT

Saturday 1:00 p.m., Mill Pond House

A small two-story wood-framed house overlooked the inlet in Centerport. The blue wooden plaque in front read Mill Pond House, Seafood Kitchen and Bar. Holly entered the airy brightly-lit dining room. There was a view of the bay through the three large picture windows located across the wide-planked wood floor. Light watercolor paintings of nearby scenes scattered along the walls. White linen tablecloths covered the square wooden tables. A waitress approached. "Good afternoon. Will you be dining alone today?"

"No, there'll be two. I'm meeting someone here."

'Would you like to wait at the bar or have a seat at a table?"

"I think I'll sit out on the deck if it's open."

"Of course, it's a beautiful day."

Holly was escorted to an outside table and ordered a glass of water. Moments drifted by as she took in the scenery of the peaceful inlet. Visions of another time in her past came into her head. Living in Marblehead, Massachusetts, and enjoying the harbor views was all she could think about.

Moshe arrived, and the dream was interrupted.

"Sorry, I'm late. Long Island Expressway traffic."

"No problem. I just arrived."

The waitress approached the table.

"Good afternoon," said the waitress as she handed each of them a menu. "The special of the day is a veal cutlet Milanese with roasted fingerling potatoes and sautéed string beans. I'll give you a few minutes to decide. Meanwhile, would you care for something from the bar?"

"Oh, yes, please. I'll have an Absolut Martini with three olives," replied Holly.

"Make mine Johnny Walker Black, neat, no ice."

"Got it."

Moshe dressed in a pale blue crewneck cashmere sweater with navy blue slacks and black polished dress shoes. The long-sleeved sweater did nothing to hide his muscular arms. His short curly black hair was well-groomed. His manicured fingernails looked professionally done, although he did not look at all feminine. *He's not what I would call handsome, but for some reason, I'm attracted.*

"How's your brother?" Moshe broke the trance once again.

"Coming along."

Just then, the waitress returned with the drinks and asked if they were ready to order.

"Yes, thank you. I'm famished," said Holly. "I'll have the Maine Lobster Roll."

"One of my favorites," advised the waitress as she turned towards Moshe.

"I'll have the veal cutlet, Milanese."

"Excellent."

"What do you do, Holly?" Moshe asked.

"Good question. Let me see. I go to school, take vacations, sail, I guess anything I feel like." Holly's eyes lit up, and a smile crossed her face.

"Wow, no work. You must be rich," Moshe said with a smile.

"Well, I guess I am. I lived in Marblehead, Massachusetts, before my partner and I while on vacation in Roatan, found a map. A treasure map. It had the location of a Spanish treasure ship off the coast of Florida. We split the proceeds. It was enough that I don't have to work. Instead, I am working on a master's degree in Art History at the Rhode Island School of Design. What about you?"

"I work at JFK Airport for a worldwide freight handling company. We offload and load cargo aircraft for various airlines. We also provide warehousing services, too."

"It seems to pay well," said Holly.

"I do well enough," said Moshe, trying to change the subject, "but I would like to hear more about why you think this wasn't an accident."

Holly explained that her brother was a cautious person and would not do something that reckless. There was no way he would be that close to the yacht, and now they are trying to say he was drunk. Never.

"Well, I agree with you. In the last couple of weeks, Stepan had been acting strangely. I think something was bothering him. He wasn't the same. I asked a couple of times, but he just said he was working on something. It may have nothing to do with the accident, but it could explain some irrational behavior. Has your brother been able to say anything yet?"

"No, not yet, but I hope to get him to speak tonight. Still, Jeff wouldn't have allowed Stepan to do anything stupid."

"Unless Stepan was driving. Would you mind if I joined you at the hospital tonight?"

"No, I'd like that. Meet me in the lobby at seven p.m."

Moshe called for the check.

The waitress returned with the check and handed it to Moshe.

"I got this," said Holly reaching for the check.

"Not today," answered Moshe waving the check away from Holly.

"Well, thank you."

He paid cash and left a fifty dollar tip on the table.

It was 7:10 p.m. when Moshe walked into the hospital lobby. Holly greeted him and took him to Jeff's room. Jeff was awake and talking to his mother and father.

"Jeff, this is Moshe Kaplan. He worked with Stepan."

"Hi, Jeff. How are you feeling today?" Moshe asked.

"Much better, thanks."

"Do you remember anything about the accident?"

"Very little, it happened so fast. We weren't even traveling near the yacht."

"You mean the yacht came toward you?"

"Yeah, it kept coming. We thought it would turn away, but it didn't."

"So, you were not riding any of the wakes kicked up by the boat?"

"No. It stalled. The jet ski wouldn't start," answered Jeff anxiously.

"So you were driving?"

"Yes. Of course. Why?"

"Just checking, no reason. Is there anything else you can tell me? Stepan was a close friend, and I'd like to know."

"Funny, as it got closer, we could see the pilot. Stepan thought he looked familiar."

"That's it?"

"That's all I can remember now."

"Thanks. That helps."

They changed the subject to something lighter. John advised of the other family members who had called to wish Jeff a speedy recovery. Finally, they decided to leave and let Jeff get some rest, promising to return the next morning. As they left the room, Jeff called to Moshe.

"Wait. I remember something else. Just before the yacht struck us, Stepan yelled, 'I know him. That's…' I never heard the ending."

Veal Cutlets Milanese Recipe

Yield: 4

Ingredients

1 pound veal cutlets, pounded thin

2 eggs

1 teaspoon salt

½ cup flour

2 cups seasoned bread crumbs

2 tablespoons olive oil

2 tablespoons butter

1 sliced lemon

Instructions

1. Lightly beat the eggs with the salt in a deep dish and spread the flour and the breadcrumbs out on separate plates. Dredge veal slices in the flour, shaking off any excess. Then dip in the egg and breadcrumbs making sure both sides are well coated with breadcrumbs.

2. Heat olive oil and butter in a large sauté pan over medium heat. Add the breaded cutlets to the pan without crowding (if you have to, you can work in batches). Cook, turning once for about 6 minutes total until golden brown and crispy. Transfer to warm plates, garnish with lemon slices and serve.

CHAPTER NINE

Moshe Kaplan, five years earlier

Moshe had begun his career in the Israeli Military. He was assigned to the elite Ayeret (reconnaissance unit) of the Israel Defense Forces (IDF). After several successful assignments, he enlisted into the Mossad (Israel Institute for Intelligence and Special Operations), where he was a part of the Kidon, an elite command of experts in infiltrating and sabotage as well as reportedly being responsible for 2,700 assassinations.

In September of 2014, Moshe had infiltrated an ISIS regiment. His assignment was relaying information back to the American-led forces about the location of the heads of ISIS, especially Abu Baka al-Baghdadi. This ISIS force had overrun an Iraqi Military outpost, thirty miles west of Baghdad. It was a massacre. Many Iraqi soldiers died that day, some by Moshe. He did not like being part of the killing, but he had to keep his cover. It was the part of the job he disliked the most. ISIS had managed to capture 200 Iraqi soldiers alive and scheduled them for execution. Included in the captives was an American with the CIA. His name was Jonathan Long.

The ISIS command had attempted to behead one of the Iraqi soldiers as a statement of what its soldiers could expect if they tried to defect. They lined up the Iraqi prisoners. Two ISIS soldiers pulled one of the Iraqi prisoners from the line and forced him to his knees. Another ISIS member dressed in black approached the prisoner and slit his throat, blood spilled out. But the sword had not severed the head, and it took a sawing action to complete the task. Moshe turned and threw up.

If the ISIS interrogators had identified Long as a westerner, Moshe knew they would torture him for information. Information that there was a spy in the ISIS ranks. Although Long did not know Moshe, he would reveal Israel's role in the fighting. Moshe had no choice. He would either eliminate Long or help him escape. After the beheading, he chose the latter.

That night during a guard change, Moshe was able to eradicate the two guards. He stripped one of the guards and handed the garments to Jonathan.

Now posing as two ISIS soldiers, Moshe and Long made their escape. Traveling off the roads and mostly at night, it took a week of hiding before they were able to enter Baghdad safely.

The fight with ISIS continued for Moshe.

Sunday 1:00 p.m., JFK Airport

Moshe was driving back to the airport along Rockaway Boulevard after lunch at the Bay House Restaurant. As he neared, the approach lights were blinking, indicating the flight path for the arriving airplanes. He saw the monster approaching. Its wings cast shadows over the fourteen cars ahead. He counted the twenty-eight wheels needed to keep this tremendous hunk of aluminum from disintegrating on impact. The wheels screeched as they hit the pavement with its weight of 385,000 pounds, not including the 300,000 pounds of freight on board. Puffs of smoke appeared from the wheels as she touched down and sped to the end of the runway.

The Antonov AN124 pulled up to the back of the cargo facility as Moshe arrived. The sign on the four-story building said Ground Services of America. They handled the ground services for several airlines, including loading and unloading of cargo, bags, and mail. Also, they did warehousing and distribution of freight. The round-the-clock operation required 240 employees.

As Moshe walked toward the back, he passed the materials handling system, which loaded, transported, and stored large aircraft cargo metal pallets. The pallets are called Unit Load Devices or ULDs. Loaded with cargo, the ULDs can weigh up to 25,000 pounds each. The internal system of the lower deck could only accommodate small ULDs no larger than 80 inches in length, 61 inches wide and 64 inches high. An outside storage area handled ULDs up to 240 inches in length, 96 inches wide and 120 inches in height.

At the rear of the building was the cargo ramp area, used for parking the various aircraft off the taxiway. GSA could accommodate three aircraft simultaneously. But today's AN124 would be using all three spaces.

Today's offload included one massive earth-moving machine which was on lease to an excavation company. The bulldozer required a licensed heavy equipment driver to drive it off the aircraft. There were an additional four ULDs, 125x96x96 inches, carrying micro quadcopters. These tiny toy drones could fit in the palm of your hand and were used for entertainment by both children and adults. Some people used them to check on areas otherwise impossible to see.

As Moshe watched, the massive aircraft's nose started to open slowly. With the top hinged to the fuselage, the bottom began moving away from the fuselage and up into the air. The immense interior (118 feet long, 24 feet wide, and 14 feet high) of this monster was exposed. Once the gate opened, the front wheels began to retract back into the fuselage, lowering the aircraft as if the plane were kneeling. Finally, a ramp appeared from inside the plane. The ramp and the hydraulics started the unfolding process as it protruded from the aircraft and laid itself onto the ground. After about twenty minutes, they were ready to unload the plane. The GSA personnel walked onto the ramp and released the tie-down straps that were holding the earthmover securely in place. A driver from the excavation company climbed on the machine and cautiously drove it off the aircraft down the aircraft's ramp. Next, GSA staff on large forklifts drove up the ramp and removed the four ULDs. They were then placed on the material handling system and stored outside the warehouse, awaiting U.S. Customs clearance and pickup.

Moshe looked up to the building from the ramp. Someone from GSA headquarters was looking down at the process from the upper office window. *He is here for the Antonov aircraft. I wonder why,* wondered Moshe.

When his shift ended, he punched out and left the building. He walked across the street to his parked black 1997 Mercedes SL500. Once inside, he reached for his cell phone.

"How about dinner?" Moshe asked.

"I'd love to. Can you make it to Newport?" answered Holly, laughing.

"What are you doing in Newport?"

"I live here. I had to clean up some things. I'll be back Monday morning. I have a meeting with a lawyer in Manhattan."

"Want some company? I'm off."

"Sure. We could have lunch in the city. Why don't I pick you up on my way? How's 11:00 a.m.?"

"Works for me. See you then."

"Oh, wait, where do you live?"

"Shore Crest Towers, 3000 Ocean Blvd. Brighton Beach. I'll meet you out front."

"OK, see you." Holly hung up.

CHAPTER TEN

Monday, 11:00 A.M.

Moshe was waiting in front of the Shore Crest Towers. *This woman intrigues me. I must get to know her better.* Just then, Holly pulled up in her BMW. Moshe opened the door and entered the car.

"Good morning. Anything new with Jeff?" he asked.

"No. Mom and dad went to see him this morning."

"Where would you like to have lunch?"

"I was thinking about Patsy's Italian Restaurant. I'm dying for some good New York-style pizza," answered Holly.

After a thirty-minute drive through midday traffic, and a short ride through the Lincoln Tunnel, they arrived in Manhattan.

Holly located a parking garage near Park Avenue and 59th Street. Moshe hailed a taxi, and Holly directed the driver to 236 W. 56th Street. A few minutes later, they pulled up to Patsy's.

They entered beneath the red awning. A small table was available in the back. Moshe guided Holly to the table and pulled out her chair.

"Thank you, I'm glad chivalry is still in vogue," said Holly.

"It is where I come from," answered Moshe.

"I love the music."

"It's the theme from the *Godfather* movie. Isn't it?"

"Yes. The first one," said Holly, "It's called *Come Softly*. Al Martino sang it."

"This place seems quite old."

"Patsy's has been an Italian favorite for over 75 years. My parents would take us at Christmas. First, we went to see the tree in Rockefeller Center, then ice skating, and finally here for pizza. It is my father's favorite place."

Moshe looked at the pictures on the walls. "I know most of the celebrities like Frank Sinatra, but I don't recognize the one in the corner," said Moshe pointing to one of the photos.

"Oh. That's an early photo of Billy Joel."

"I never saw him that young."

A waiter came over.

"Welcome to Patsy's. Do you want to see a menu?"

"No," answered Holly, "we'll have a large cheese pizza. Extra crispy with olive oil."

"No problem, there's oil on the table," said the waiter picking up a bottle from between the condiments. "Would you care for a cocktail from the bar?"

"Do you have bottled water?" asked Holly.

"Of course. We have Aqua Panna or San Pellegrino sparkling water."

"I'll have the San Pellegrino," answered Holly.

"Make that two."

"So, how was your trip back to Rhode Island?" Moshe inquired.

"It went well. I just had to talk to my teachers about making up some classes while I'm down here. I also met with a close friend of mine, Castle Rock. He's one of my friends who shared in the sunken treasure. I would never have been able to get this lawyer without his help."

The pizza arrived. It was crispy with a charred bottom, thin and oily. Holly picked up a slice, and the melted mozzarella cheese stretched across her plate.

"Just the way I like it," she remarked, "as they made it in the old days with the brick ovens. You can't get pizza like this at the newer restaurants."

Moshe took a slice and bit into it. Suddenly he opened his mouth and grabbed for the glass of water.

"Hot!" He mumbled.

Holly just laughed.

They continued eating in silence until the pie was gone.

"How long have you worked for Ground Services?"

"A little over a year."

What did you do before?"

Moshe did not like where the conversation was going.

"What time is your appointment?" he asked, looking down at his watch.

"Two-thirty."

"Then, I think we should finish up and leave."

The waiter brought the bill, and Holly reached for it, but Moshe was faster. He paid in cash.

Outside, Moshe hailed another taxi and asked Holly for the address.

"665 Park Avenue," Holly instructed the driver.

They entered the building and walked up to the security guard.

"How can I help you?" asked the guard.

"I have an appointment with Samuel Baum."

"Sixteenth floor, elevators to your right."

They took the elevator to the sixteenth floor. Baum and Belkin occupied the entire story. A woman wearing a navy blue Anne Taylor suit sat behind the only desk in the lobby. Her black hair had streaks of grey. Dark red lipstick and black eyeliner accentuated her pale face. Behind the woman were two opaque glass doors with "Baum and Belkin" stenciled in gold lettering.

"How may I help you?" requested the receptionist.

"I'm Holly Flynn. I have a two-thirty appointment with Samuel Baum."

"Oh yes, Miss Flynn. Go right in. Mr. Baum is waiting for you. He's in the office on the left."

"Thank you," replied Holly, and Moshe opened the door for her. "I'll wait for you out here."

"No, please come."

She entered the office on the left and Samuel was hanging up the phone when he got up from his desk and walked towards her.

"I'm so glad to meet you, Ms. Flynn, finally. Cas has told me so much about you. He thinks you are one of the most amazing people he knows and contributes his success to your resourcefulness." Samuel extended his hand to Holly.

"Well, thank you, Mr. Baum, but it was a team effort. I have some amazing friends in Boston."

"First, please call me Sam. Let's sit over here by the coffee table."

They strolled over to the table.

"What have you got for me today?" inquired Holly, trying to keep from shaking. "Oh! By the way, this is my friend, Moshe. He's my support."

"Nice to meet you, Moshe."

They took seats around a rectangular oak coffee table. Holly and Moshe sat on the settee and Samuel in an armchair.

"Can I offer you a cup of tea or coffee?"

"No, thanks. We just finished lunch."

He laid the folder on the table. It was titled, Jeff Flynn. He opened the folder and took out the first document.

"Here's a copy of the hospital report from the examination when he first arrived." He handed a copy to Holly.

"It notes traces of alcohol in his blood, but it is below the point of intoxication. I believe the DA is going to try to sway the jury into thinking it was higher at the time of the accident. I'm not worried about that. She won't get away with it."

Samuel then handed Holly a second report. "This is the report from the investigating officer at the scene. It describes the boat and jet ski and your brother's condition at the time. The most damning part is the statement from the boat pilot. He states that your brother was the driver and that he was driving erratically. The report also says the pilot tried to avoid the jet ski, but Jeff continued with his erratic behavior, and finally drove directly into the yacht."

Holly's face turned bright red. She jumped up from her seat and screamed, "That's a lie."

"Of course, I don't believe it, Holly, but we need to see what we are up against. I still think their case is weak. What can you tell me? I heard Jeff is getting better."

Holly composed herself. "He's able to talk and remembers seeing the yacht. Jeff remembers that Stepan was saying he wished he could afford such a yacht and wanted to take a closer look. They started toward the yacht when the engine stalled. He could not start the engine. The yacht was coming directly toward them. They tried to wave it off, but it kept coming. Like it *wanted* to crash into them."

"Well, we'll have to find out why the pilot would go after the jet ski."

"What about my brother's bail hearing?"

"We'll take care of that. I'm sure the bail will be low, as this was not intentional. He has a good job at the bank and owns his condo. He doesn't appear to be at risk of leaving the area or the country."

Holly stood up and grabbed Samuel's hand. "I'm leaving my brother in your hands, Sam. Help him, please!"

"I will."

They left the building, and Moshe offered to take Holly to dinner at Taras Bulba's, a Ukrainian restaurant on Broadway. She accepted and they hailed a taxi. Moshe directed the taxi to take Broadway to downtown. He could not remember the address and the driver was not familiar with the restaurant. Finally, he spotted the small red brick building with the red awning and small tables out front in the middle of the block.

A man with a long mustache and wearing a red wool Cossack coat greeted them. The coat had a long slit up the back, with gold braids as ornaments on the front. His low-heeled black leather boots came up to just below his knees. With a large round black fur hat upon his head, he needed to stoop down to enter the doorway.

Russian and Ukrainian antiques from rural farmhouses filled the small room. There were sketches of Cossacks and Taras Bulba on the whitewashed stucco walls. They located a small wooden farm table in the rear. A traditional Ukrainian band, consisting of a flute player, accordionist, bass drummer, and singer were playing Russian folk songs in the front.

A waitress dressed in a white peasant blouse with embroidered flowers on the front and a long red skirt, came over to take their order. She had a wreath of flowers in her hair.

"Welcome to Taras Bulba's. What can I get you?" she said in a Russian accent, which may have been faked.

"Can I see your wine list, please?"

"Of course," answered the waitress as she reached over and removed one from a nearby table.

Moshe scanned the wines and decided on a red.

"A bottle of the Argentine Malbec," requested Moshe.

"Are you ready to order?"

"Not yet," answered Moshe. "We need to see a menu."

The waitress returned with the Malbec and an overly-large menu.

After removing the cork, she poured a small portion into Moshe's glass. He took a sip and nodded his approval. The waitress filled their glasses.

"I'll give you some time to look over our menu. Meanwhile, our specials tonight are a potato soup, grilled wild salmon, and homemade kovbasy," said the waitress as she left.

Holly scanned the menu. The cover had a picture of the imposing Taras Bulba.

"So who was this Taras Bulba?" Holly asked.

"Taras Bulba was the main character in a historical novella by Nikolai Gogol. It's a story about the life of an old Zaporozhian Cossack and his two sons, Andrii and Ostap," Moshe continued. "He is based on several historical personalities."

"Tell me more."

"It's boring. But there is a movie you can rent."

"Now, I remember. I think Yul Brenner was in it."

"That's the one."

The waitress returned for their order.

Moshe ordered for both.

"We'll start with an order of Pelmeni[2], then two cups of borscht, and, for our main course, we'll have the Golubtsy[3]."

The waitress departed to place the order. Holly removed the papers from her handbag. She looked over the hospital report. There was nothing there, nothing that would help Jeff. Then she took out the witness statement. As she reread the pilot's description of the event, her heart began beating rapidly, and a cold sweat made her hands clammy. She started reading it aloud.

"The jet ski was jumping the waves behind the boat. Then they came around and tried to jump my side wake. They turned and

---

[2] Moon shaped light dough filled with chopped meats.
[3] Ukrainian stuffed cabbage.

headed straight for my boat. Statement from yacht pilot, Pavio Kravets. It continues with…"

"Hold it," demanded Moshe. "Let me see that."

Holly handed over the report to Moshe, and he started looking over the document. She looked questioningly at him. Moshe continued through the description and looked back at Holly.

"I found something."

"What? Tell me," Holly demanded.

"I know this name."

"What name?"

"Pavio Kravets."

Just then, their order arrived. They were famished and started eating, putting Pavio Kravets on hold for the moment.

Later the waitress came by and asked if they would like some dessert or coffee. Moshe looked around and realized they were the last couple in the restaurant. He looked down at his wrist. It was eleven p.m.

Moshe apologized, "Oh, I'm so sorry. I didn't realize how late it was."

"No problem, we enjoyed watching you two enjoying each other."

Holly blushed.

"Thank you, I'll take the check please," said Moshe.

She returned with the check which Moshe paid in cash. He helped Holly from the table and turned. He reached in his wallet and slipped the waitress a 100 dollar bill as they left.

Pelmeni Recipe
Ingredients
3 cups all-purpose flour
1 tsp salt
1 large egg
1 cup of cold water
1 pound extra-lean ground beef
1 pound extra lean ground pork
2 medium onions
4 cloves of garlic
1/4 cup water
1/2 bunch flat-leaf parsley
1/2 bunch dill
1 teaspoon salt
1 teaspoon pepper
2 bay leaves
2 tablespoon butter, sour cream, fresh dill or parsley

Instructions
1. In a food processor, pulse flour and salt. With the motor running, add the egg through the tube and then cold water. Let the processor do its work for a minute until the dough forms around the blade.

2. Transfer the dough into a bowl, cover with a tea towel and let it sit for 30 minutes.

3. Meanwhile, make the meat filling by combining beef, pork, salt, and pepper. Then in a food processor blend onions, garlic, parsley, dill and water and add to the meat mixture.

4. Use your hands to combine well, then pinch a small amount off and form a meatball. Fry the meatball and taste it for the right

combination of salt and spices in your filling. Adjust spices if necessary.

5. Divide the dough into quarters and form the quarters into balls.

6. Take one dough ball and roll it out on a well-floured surface in a thin sheet approximately 1/16" in thickness. Keep the rest of the dough covered to avoid drying out.

7. Cut out circles with a 2" to 3" cookie or scone cutter. Put a teaspoonful of meat filling into each dough circle, slightly off-center, fold the dough over to form a half-moon shape and pinch the edges shut with your fingertips. If you want a more attractive look, go over the edge one more time and this time pinch the edges together using your two fingers and a thumb and twist them to form a ruffled edge.

8. Repeat with the remaining dough circles until you run out of dough and meat.

9. Set aside the necessary amount of pelmeni for dinner and freeze the rest in a well-floured, air-tight container to prevent sticking.*

10. Bring a large pot of water to a boil, add salt and 2 bay leaves. Drop pelmeni into rapidly boiling water and stir to prevent them from sticking to the bottom. Once they float to the top, cook for ten more minutes.

11. Drain pelmeni and pour melted butter over them. Gently stir or toss to coat.

12. Serve with sour cream and chopped fresh dill or parsley.

* Do not thaw frozen pelmeni before cooking. They should be boiled frozen for fifteen minutes.

CHAPTER ELEVEN

Shore Crest Towers, 11:45 p.m.

Moshe opened the door of the BMW.

"Aren't you going to invite me in for a nightcap? You can't leave me hanging like this. What do you know about this, Pavio guy?" Holly demanded.

Moshe perceived Holly's displeasure by her raised eyebrows. "OK. Park the car and come in. We'll talk."

Moshe's apartment was on the seventh floor overlooking Raritan Bay. The apartment was painted a subtle white with a dark oak floor. All the stainless steel appliances were up to date. A king-size bed and one dresser for the bedroom. One sofa and chair in the living room. A small dining table with two chairs and a sixty-inch TV completed the accessories. The apartment had a contemporary European flare, minimalistic but tastefully expensive.

Holly contemplated what she was seeing. *Moshe isn't into furniture, but I wonder how he can afford this apartment on a warehouseman's salary. There must be something more to Mr. Kaplan. The man who acts so reassured as if nothing could surprise him — one who knows his strengths and weaknesses and accepts both.*

Moshe placed two wine glasses on the small table. He opened a wine refrigerator under the counter and chose a bottle of chilled white wine. After uncorking the bottle of Coup de Foudre, a sauvignon blanc from Napa, Moshe poured two glasses and handed one to Holly.

"Sorry, this is all I have at this time. Wasn't expecting company," he said jokingly.

Holly took a sip. "This is good. You must have bought it for someone special."

"I bought it to celebrate a yet-to-be-completed assignment."

"What is it?"

"Nothing. Let's talk about Jeff's problem."

"OK, so who is Pavio?"

"Pavio Kravets works for Mykhailo Chernov. Chernov owns Lyresa Enterprises, Inc., an import company. Lyresa is also the name of Chernov's yacht. It's named after his wife. Lyresa Enterprises also owns an interest in GSA, Ground Services of America, an airfreight handling company, my current employer. Stepan was also employed there before his demise."

"Then, there is a connection here."

"Yes, I believe it was a wet job."

"What?" asked Holly, her eyebrows drawn together.

"Sorry, a target hit."

"But why?"

"That's what we have to find out. I need your help."

"Sure, anything I can do to clear my brother."

"Stepan argued with his wife's cousin, Alexi, at a party a couple of weeks ago. I overheard it. They were talking Russian, thinking I would not know what they were talking about. But, I made out that they were arguing about some shipment arriving. I now think Pavio was involved."

"You speak Russian?"

"Yes, read and write also, but I keep that a secret. It allows me to eavesdrop on conversations."

"Any other languages?" Holly quizzed.

"Well, yes. Yiddish, Spanish, and Arabic, it's kind of a hobby."

"You always surprise me. Any other secrets you'd like to share?" asked Holly.

"Not at the moment," Moshe answered with a smile.

"What do you want me to do?"

"I want you to come to the warehouse as my guest and distract Pavio so I can search his office."

"Shouldn't we just tell the police?"

"They would need a search warrant and a better reason than my guess. The police have rules. I don't," Moshe continued, "Pavio would be alerted. Trust me on this. I'm going to prove your brother is innocent."

"You really can do this?" Holly pumped Moshe nervously.

"Yes, I can." Moshe's smile disappeared from his mouth. His eyes squinted, and his brows lowered, his lips tightened.

Holly agreed to assist in any way possible.

They finished the wine, and Holly went into her purse and pulled out her cell.

"Give me a second. Let me call my mother. She's a worrywart and it's late for her."

"Of course."

"Hi, Mom. How's Jeff? Good. Yes, the meeting with the lawyer went well. I'll tell you all about it tomorrow. Listen, I'm staying at a friend's tonight. I'll meet you at the hospital. Love you too." She hung up.

A surprised look came over Moshe's face. He was not used to being surprised.

"I'm not used to having guests, as you can see. There's only one bed."

"It fits two, doesn't it?" she answered.

"I think we need another bottle of wine," said Moshe as he went to the refrigerator.

He poured them both a glass. After pacing around the room in silence, he took a seat beside Holly.

"Holly, I hope you don't feel you owe me anything for my help?"

"Oh! No, I don't want to be home tonight." Holly took his hand in hers and gave it a slight squeeze. "Thank you. That was very thoughtful."

"I don't expect anything." Moshe continued, "I don't want to jeopardize our relationship."

"You won't," said Holly as she leaned over and kissed him.

The kiss was returned.

Moshe picked her up in his arms and carried her into the bedroom. "Is this the usual way you meet people?"

"I haven't met anyone who made me feel like this in over two years."

Holly started unbuttoning her blouse, and it dropped to the floor. Her bra was next. She was waiting for Moshe to react.

"Am I being too aggressive?" Holly whispered in a deep seductive voice.

"No, but it has been a couple of years for me, also," answered Moshe, as he took off his shirt and unbuckled his pants.

They both fell naked on top of the bed. No time to pull down the blanket. He kissed her gently and caressed her breast. She snuggled up to him. They fell asleep in each other's arms.

She was awakened the next morning by the smell of strong coffee. A wide-awake Moshe came out of the shower wearing just a towel wrapped around his waist. He sat beside Holly on the bed, looking out the window into the bay. There were scars along his back.

Holly placed her hand on his back and felt the deep scars.

"How did you get those scars?" she asked.

"Too long a story. Why? Do they bother you? I can put a shirt on."

"No! Of course not. I'm just curious."

"Why are you not married? You are an attractive woman. Or are you divorced?"

"Neither, I have been with men before and was kind of serious with one, in particular, a few years back. We lived together but we never talked about the future. It was serious but we both knew it was only for the moment. We came into a large sum of money and found we both had other ambitions. He opened a successful art gallery in Boston and I went back to college. We are still good friends and talk frequently but the romance was gone long ago. I have my own life ahead of me and I want to see where it goes. Marriage will come in time, I suppose, but I don't see it as a necessity."

"This Castle guy?"

"Yes."

"Holly, when I made love to you, it felt like the first time. You drew me in with an innocence I have never experienced with another woman."

Holly looked up at him and tossed the sheet off the bed, revealing her naked body.

"Come back to bed and after we'll take a shower together and have coffee," said Holly reaching out her hand.

He dropped the towel.

Tuesday, 9:00 a.m.

Pavio Kravets walked into Lyresa Enterprises, Inc. on Rockaway Blvd. in Jamaica, New York. Mykhailo Chernov's office was on the fourth floor. Pavio took the elevator. Mykhailo was behind his desk with his elbows on the counter, and his right hand pressed against his forehead. He was deep in thought. Alexi was seated across from him. Pavio walked in.

"You fucked up, Pavio. I sent to scare Stepan off, not kill him. He has many friends. I hope this fuckup does not affect our plans."

"I can take care of myself and everything else."

"Is everything else going as planned?" demanded Mykhailo in Russian.

"Yes. Stepan's funeral went as expected, no issues. The District Attorney believes the guy with Stepan was responsible for the accident. The police released the Lyresa, and it is now moored at the Brooklyn Marina," continued Pavio in Russian.

"What about the shipment?"

"We are on schedule," answered Pavio.

"Good, keep me advised. Now leave, as I have business with Alexi." Pavio rose from his seat, and Mykhailo looked to Alexi but said nothing. There was no handshake as Pavio left the office.

Mykhailo stood up and walked over to the window. Alexi just sat quietly, waiting. Finally, Mykhailo returned to his seat.

Mykhailo started the conversation once he was sure Pavio had left the building. "Alexi, we must be careful with fucking Pavio. He is getting too reckless, taking actions on his own without my permission."

"I know. He thinks he is untouchable."

"I would have gotten rid of that fucking bastard a long time ago, but he has connections overseas. He better watch his ass if this thing gets out of hand. Perhaps he is looking to replace me. "

"I assure you that will not happen," promised Alexi.

"What about the girl. She seems to be getting involved. Why is she around? What is she looking for?" inquired a concerned Mykhailo.

"Leave the girl to me. I will take care of her," offered Alexi.

"I leave it in your hands, Alexi."

"All accounts will be settled. I promise," assured Alexi as he left the office.

Tuesday 11:00 a.m.

Holly arrived at Stony Brook University Hospital. During the drive from Moshe's to the hospital, something kept creeping into her mind. It had nagged at her the entire trip.

Before going to see Jeff, she bought a cup of coffee and sat at a table. She was looking into the deep dark liquid and thinking:

Where does Moshe get his money? The apartment, the expensive wine, the check paying, and of course, the tipping. His extravagant lifestyle is not possible on an average salary. Something else is supplementing his income. Is he part of a criminal family?

She once again dialed Cas.

"Gallery 21. This is Cas, how can I help you?"

"Cas, its Holly."

"How did it go with the lawyer?"

"Great, but that's not why I called."

"Go ahead."

"You're the only one I can talk to about this."

"OK, what's the problem?"

"I met this guy at the funeral for Jeff's friend. The one that died in the accident. He was charming and offered to help me. He showed an interest in the case. So, I befriended him. We've gone out to lunch and dinner, and he accompanied me to the lawyers."

"So, what's your problem?"

"He's too good to be true."

"I don't get it."

"Last night, I went to his apartment. He has a great apartment, costly furniture, although a few pieces, and he drinks expensive wines. When we go to dinner, he always picks up the check and leaves large cash tips, usually fifties and hundreds. He works at the airport for a freight handling company. There's no way he could afford to be this extravagant on his salary. I'm afraid there is something else. He thinks Jeff and his friend were targeted. Perhaps he is into something illegal. Cas, I trust you. Do I imagine things?"

"OK, what's his name?"

"Moshe Kaplan."

"OK, that's a start. What else do you know about him?"

"He lives at the Shore Crest Towers, 3000 Ocean Boulevard in Brighton Beach, and works for Ground Services America at JFK."

"I think you kinda like this guy."

"More than that, I'm afraid."

"Alright, I'll get right on it and call you back in a day or two."

"Thanks, Cas."

"You're welcome."

She continued into the hospital.

The ICU nurse explained that Jeff was recovering nicely and was moved out of ICU into a regular room. She checked the computer and gave Holly the new room number.

Her mother and father were already in the room, talking to Jeff. She smiled and walked up to Jeff and kissed him on the cheek.

"How're you feeling today?"

"Great. The doctor says I'll be able to leave by the end of the week."

"Do you remember anything else from the accident?"

"No, just what I already told you."

"What about the warrant for his arrest?" Pat inquired impatiently.

"I met with the lawyer yesterday. He said the bail should be no problem as Jeff is not a risk to leave the area."

"What about the charges?" Holly's father continued with the questions.

"He felt the intoxication was a non-issue and for us not to worry about that. The only case the DA has is the statement from the boat pilot that they ran into him. We need to find a reason for the opposite, that the pilot was actually after Jeff and Stepan."

"Can he do that?"

"I don't think so, but Moshe says he can."

John made one hand into a fist and was rubbing it with the other when he asked, "How?"

"Moshe says there is a connection between the boat pilot and the people Stepan worked for."

"That would be a strange coincidence," commented Pat.

"I remember Stepan was trying to say he knew him just before we crashed," offered an excited Jeff.

"I'm doing some research that Moshe asked me to do. Hopefully, I'll find the connection to all this. Meanwhile, I may not be around as much, but I'll call every day to see how things are going."

"Whatever you need to do to clear this up," offered John.

Holly kissed Jeff, her mother, and father, and left.

Holly drove to the Port Jefferson Library. She sifted through every business journal she could find looking for information on Ground Services of America. After an hour of failing to find anything, she stepped up to the information desk.

"Hi, can I help you?" offered the grey-haired woman at the information desk.

"Yes, I hope so. I'm looking for information on a freight handling company called Ground Services of America doing business internationally and in the U.S.," Holly continued, "but I don't know where to look."

"I'm sorry. You probably would need *The Directory of Importers and Exporters,*" replied the librarian, "but, unfortunately, our small budget is unable to afford every reference book."

"Where can I find a copy?"

"Check the internet first. If you don't find what you're looking for there, I'm sure you can find it at The Manhattan Public Library on Thirty-fourth Street and Fifth Avenue."

"Thanks. I will."

Holly went out to her car and retrieved her IPad. She found a table in a quiet area of the library and began her search.

She received a hit.

GSA-Ground Services of America is part of a worldwide cargo ground handling system with affiliates in Russia and Ukraine. The CEO and Board Chairman of GSA is Mykhailo Chernov.

She decided to check on the affiliates.

The Russian affiliate was named Ground Services of Russia or GSR. The CEO and Board Chairman was a Vasili Petrov. Then she noticed another member of the board, Mykhailo Chernov. She recognized Vasili Petrov as being on the board of GSA.

One more time, she checked for Ground Services of Ukraine, (GSU). The CEO and Board Chairman was Ivan Kushnir. Again Mykhailo was listed as a board member.

Mykhailo was associated with both of these companies.

She called Moshe to tell him what she had found.

"Hi Holly, I was going to call you. Last night was the best night I've had in a very long time."

"For me too." She went on to explain what she had found.

"Good work, but that will not clear Jeff. Those names are all mafia. Vasili Petrov is the head of the Russian Mafia. Ivan Kushnir is head of the Ukrainian Mafia. It looks like Mykhailo is also mafia. But we still need a reason why they would want to kill Stepan," explained Moshe.

"What about if I research the names and find out what other companies they may be affiliated with?"

"That might work. It's worth a try."

Holly hung up. Once again, she pulled out her IPad and searched. Mykhailo Chernov came back with several hits. Ukrainian Cargo Transport, YBT, IATA two-letter code YT, numeric designator 666, which was a Ukrainian cargo airline operating four Antonov AN124 aircraft, was the first. A second hit came up with Lyresa Enterprises, Inc., a holding company for some other smaller companies, including Lyresa Imports, an importing company specializing in toy drone helicopters, headquartered at JFK Airport in New York.

It was getting late, so she called Moshe. She explained what she had found.

"It seems he is into everything. His hands are definitely not clean, but it doesn't prove anything. We'll have to break into Pavio's office tomorrow and hope to find more incriminating evidence."

"Wait, there is one other company. Kharkiv Technical Center (KTC)."

"KTC. They're into artificial intelligence technology. Dangerous high tech. That's one that scares me. They had a contract with the Russian military to research robotics for LAWs."

"LAWs?" Holly was shaking her head

"Lethal Autonomous Weapons Systems. Check your IPad."

"I found it," said Holly a moment later. "You're right, listen to this. *Lethal autonomous weapons (LAWs) are a type of military robot designed to select and attack military targets (people, installations) without intervention by a human operator. LAWs are also called lethal autonomous weapons systems (LAWS), robotic weapons, or killer robots. LAWs may operate in the air, on land, on water, or under water.*"

Moshe explained, "KTR had a contract to develop some kind of LAWs to use in urban areas that would target enemy forces and alleviate the danger of Russian troops going into buildings and enclosed areas. After ten years of research and three test failures, Russia canceled the contract with KTR."

"That's bad stuff," answered Holly as her mouth dropped.

"Very bad. That's why I have to get into Pavio's office."

"OK. I was afraid of that. What time?"

"The Antonov flight is coming in at 1:30 p.m. tomorrow. Pavio will be in tomorrow. You can distract him while I search his office. Why don't we meet for lunch?"

"When and where?"

"Eleven thirty at the Bay House."

"Where's that?"

"It's by the airport in Rosedale at 155 Bayview Ave. off of Rockaway Boulevard. Dress casually but seductively. I need you to be the center of attention."

"Got it. I know just what to wear, and I'll use my GPS to locate the Bay House."

"See you tomorrow at the Bay House."

CHAPTER TWELVE

December 1979 Democratic Republic of Afghanistan

T he explosion at half-past six on the evening of Thursday, 27 December 1979, could be felt all over Kabul. It signaled the launch of what would be the climax of Hafizullah Amin's abbreviated term as President of Afghanistan. He would not live out the night.

September 14, 1979, Afghan President Nur Muhammad Tariki was killed by supporters of Hafizullah Amin. Amin, with the backing of the Soviet Union, became President, and during his first three months in office, tried to win the support of those who revolted against Tariki. This action led to the regime's harshest measures, including the execution of thousands of Afghans.

It did not take long for the Soviets to realize there must be a regime change if they wanted to keep their twenty-year friendship with Afghanistan. His Soviet supporters betrayed Amin, and this is how it began.

At Amin's request, on 25 December, the Soviet Union began sending in the 42nd Army and Air Force troops to protect his regime. But this was the beginning of Operation Storm-333, the assassination of Amin.

Amin was having a luncheon earlier on the evening of 27 December for guests to view the newly renovated Tapa-e-Tajbcg palace. Many had been taken ill after the meal and were sent to the nearby Soviet-built hospital. A Soviet KGB sleeper agent had been installed as the head chef for the palace. He contaminated the food with an unknown substance. Amin, himself, was ill but chose to have his regular Soviet doctor treat him at home. This was part of the Soviet plan to remove Amin and his regime.

At approximately twenty minutes past seven on December 27, a rocket attack began shelling Tajbeg. The rockets were a signal for the operation to begin. A Soviet armored unit consisting of 5000 men began moving from Kabul International Airport, causing the earth to shake. Amin called in the head of his palace guards, Commander Jahandad, who advised him they were under attack by the Soviet Union.

"The Soviets are our comrades. They are here at my request. It must be Tariki's followers," said Amin.

"I don't believe that. My agents have surveillance on the Soviet Embassy and spotted some of your former party members, including Asadullah Sarwari secretly entering it," insisted Jahandad.

"Regardless, you must protect the palace."

"Of course. I have three tanks and 1800 guards ready to give their lives for you."

"I knew I could trust you, my friend."

Jahandad left, never to see Amin again.

All roads to the palace were secured by mines except one, but heavy guns and artillery defended it. The second line of defense consisted of seven posts that were handled by sentries with mortars, machine guns, and automatic rifles. The outer fortifications of the palace were secured by the three tanks and the Presidential Guard.

The Soviet troops included members of the elite Spetsgruppa A, also known as the Alpha group of the Soviet Special Forces, under the command of the KGB. The Alpha group was trained in all forms of combat and covert operations.

A twenty-four-year-old lieutenant, Mykhailo Chernov, had just been assigned as a Special Operations Officer in the elite Alpha unit. This was his first assignment. He was in charge of a team of five operatives.

Major Vasili Petrov was in command of the unit for this high-risk clandestine operation. A KGB agent had accompanied the Soviet Ambassador on a covert operation a few days before to identify the location of various rooms in the palace. A drawing of the palace interior was distributed to the Alpha unit.

On that December night, Lieutenant Chernov and his troop, dressed in Afghan uniforms, would spearhead the attack on the palace. He assembled his men who were stationed as guards in the Soviet Embassy. Mykhailo asked the commander what the rules of engagement were for this covert operation.

"We are ordered to take the Presidential Palace in Kabul, terminate Amin and his regime, and neutralize everyone. No witnesses...," answered Major Petrov.

"What about women and children?" Mykhailo asked.

"No exceptions. Are our transports here?"

"Yes, nine APCs just arrived."

"Excellent. Assemble the troops, and let's get loaded."

Mykhailo and his team entered the first of the APCs. There were five Alpha officers, one driver, and one gunner in each. It was dark when they approached the palace. Major Petrov accompanied the Alpha unit in the first APC.

As the convoy entered the road leading to the palace, the Afghan defenders began to fire artillery at the motorcade.

"Our covers blown," shouted Petrov over the shelling.

"The other troops must have failed to neutralize the communications."

"Too late to stop now. Keep going."

A loud explosion shook the transport.

"We've been hit. I can't get us moving," screamed the driver.

"Everyone out," ordered Petrov.

The men scrambled out of the vehicle, looking for some protection from the shelling.

"Mykhailo, I'm hit," yelled Petrov.

"It's not bad, but you must stay here," said Mykhailo.

"What's our situation?"

"They have disabled the first and last APCs. Our driver and gunner are injured. I have four men. But I don't have word from the last vehicle. We are targets in a shooting gallery at this moment."

"We can't stay here. Can you take your squad and neutralize that shelling?" Petrov asked.

"Yes," answered Mykhailo as he grabbed the two of the anti-tank grenade launchers from the vehicle.

"Follow me," ordered Mykhailo, pointing to the remaining men.

The men followed behind as Mykhailo scrambled into the brush on the side of the road. Then they crawled along the bottom of the dirt road away from the action.

"OK, I think we are out of range. Get up. We will flank the tanks."

As they approached the tanks, Mykhailo yelled out his orders.

"We will break into two teams. Boris, Sava, and I will take out the tank on the left," he pointed to the next two. "Lev and Foka will take the right one. Then we will both focus on the third tank. We must take out the first two together. It is now 2150 hours. We will fire at exactly 2200 hours. Let's go. Good luck."

Mykhailo, Boris, and Sava crawled along the ground toward the tank. The Afghans were too busy focusing on the Soviet troops; they did not notice the team approaching.

"Are you ready, Boris?"

"Yes."

"As soon as the tanks are disabled, we must run up and neutralize any survivors."

Mykhailo aimed and waited for Boris's signal to fire.

Boris yelled, "Fire," as he tapped Mykhailo's shoulder.

There were two spontaneous explosions. One tank left.

Five seconds later, two more explosions. No more tanks. Mykhailo's men now approached the disabled tank and eliminated any resistance. There were no prisoners or survivors.

The remainder of the convoy was now able to resume the battle.

Mykhailo radioed back to the convoy, "Fire the gas cannon at the front gate."

A moment later, an explosion of gas billowed out in front of the palace. Guards were coughing and trying to see. They were in complete chaos and easy targets for Mykhailo's men. Seconds later, the squad entered the palace. They could hear the renewed firefight behind them.

The unit made its way room by room, eliminating everyone in their path. Some had raised their hands in surrender. It made no difference.

Mykhailo and his men entered a room and found a small girl cowering in shock. One of his men prepared to neutralize the child. Mykhailo grabbed the rifle from his hand and pulled the girl aside. "Run," he shouted at the girl. She would survive this night.

They continued their search and came across heavy fire at one point. Grenades were thrown, and the guards neutralized. Boris finished them off as they passed. Mykhailo entered the next room. He fired immediately, eradicating one of the doctors.

Another doctor hiding behind a nurse yelled, "Don't shoot. I am Soviet" in Ukrainian. He lived.

"Where is Amin?" shouted Mykhailo.

The doctor pointed to a door. They stood aside and shot into the door. The door was kicked in. Amin was holding a gun but unable to fire because of the sedative the doctors had given him. The team once again opened fire. The flurry of bullets disabled Amin. Mykhailo pulled out his Zorki 4 camera and took a final picture before he fired the obligatory shot through Amin's head.

It took less than an hour to complete the mission. Any survivors who did not escape were killed. None were left to tell the tale. A total of 2400 Afghans were killed as well as two Soviet soldiers. The bodies were transported to a nearby hill and buried. Amin's bullet-riddled body was displayed to the new Soviet client state leaders. His body buried in the unmarked grave with the others. No one was allowed to enter the burial site for the duration of the war.

Mykhailo gave Petrov the film.

Major Petrov survived that day and was promoted to Colonel but was unable to continue in a combat unit. After being transferred to Moscow for reassignment, Mykhailo would stay in contact with Petrov over the years.

After the collapse of the Soviet Union, the Alpha units downgraded. Mykhailo left the military, and with a wife and child, needed employment. Petrov offered Mykhailo a position in his new organization, the Bratva (Russian mafia).

December 1, 1987, Democratic Republic of Afghanistan

Pavio Kravets, after two years in the Soviet 56th Air Guards Assault Brigade as a paratrooper, was recruited into the elite Spetsnaz sniper unit. In addition to airborne training, he was schooled in ambushing, mining and demining, sniper, and mountain climbing for another three months. His previous Sambo (Russian combat martial arts) education was an advantage, as were his communist political views. A psychological examination, which he passed, was also required.

His weapon of choice was a Soviet SVD sniper rifle, which he mastered to the extent that he was proficient at up to 1340 meters. Soon, he was assigned to a unit setting up an ambush for a group of Mujahedeen fighters. A KGB agent, Boris, had been working with this group trading Soviet arms and ammunition for drugs for over a year and had finally convinced them he was ready to defect. He traveled with them for the following six months and participated in many skirmishes in which he was forced to kill Russians. On the last raid, he was able to fake his demise and rejoin his Soviet troops. It was his knowledge of the Mujahedeen fighters' routine that led to this mission.

"OK, comrades, we will set up our ambush in the mountains overlooking the pass below. The other side of the road is a sheer drop, and there is no cover for the rebels. Our unit is dispersing over the higher side of the pass giving us the advantage of the high ground with the rebels passing below." Boris continued instructing his troops, "we will wait until the entire rebel convoy is in the position below us without any cover. The first squad will disable the first vehicle in the column and the third will disable the last. The road is too narrow for them to pass and we will have them in a trap. There will be a total of three thousand meters between the lead troops and the last. Hold your fire until I give the order."

"Pavio, you will stay by my side. I want you to eliminate Mohammed Khan personally. I will point him out to you. We will take a position in the middle of the pass. Will you be able to cover the entire pass from here? You may have to take your shot at 1400 meters."

"I will not let you down, comrade Boris," answered Pavio proudly.

The team took up their positions and waited for the rebels. The rebels always used this pass on their way to the village to acquire supplies. The villagers were pro-rebels and mostly relatives.

After what seemed an eternity, but was only a thirty-minute wait, the rebels entered the pass. They were cautious as this was the only part of their trip without cover. They came in a single file with Mohammed Khan commanding from the second jeep.

"Pavio, do you see the person alone in the back seat of the second vehicle?" inquired Boris.

"Yes," whispered Pavio.

"That's your target, wait until the last possible moment to make the kill."

Pavio aimed.

"Patience, Pavio, I want the entire column to enter the pass."

"Understood, comrade."

The rebels continued with men out front, scouting the hillside for any danger. Still, the Soviets kept their positions and held their fire. As soon as the lead group was close to reaching the end of the pass, Boris gave the order to Pavio. Pavio fired. The shot traveled close to 1400 meters. Mohammed Khan's head exploded. Heavy bursts of fire rained down on the rebels for the next twenty minutes. It did not end until all 110 insurgents were dead. The Soviet troop canvassed the area. There would be no prisoners to take back that day.

As a reward, Pavio received a Stechkin automatic pistol (APS). Although not standard equipment for a sniper, he had been able to persuade his commander to allow this extravagance after being credited with killing a Mujahideen chief commander.

Pavio enjoyed being an assassin, and he was looking forward to a rewarding future in the service; but in 1989, the Afghan war ended for the Soviets and shortly after, the Soviet Union broke up. His unit disbanded and Pavio went back to his family in Kiev. He had made some contacts in the black market while he was in Afghanistan and discussed this with some family members. One of them was Ivan Kushnir who was a Brigadier (Captain) in the Ukrainian mafia.

Ivan took on Pavio as a soldier in his mafia family. Together, with Pavio's Afghan contacts, they would move up in the organization.

Moscow 1993 Offices of GSA Russia

The man sat alone at the large table. Mykhailo did not recognize the stranger.

Mykhailo drove to the old warehouse building just outside of Sheremetyevo International Airport. He had been ordered there by his patriarch, Vasili Petrov. Mykhailo slowly walked into the room, the leather soles of his shoes echoing as he crossed the bare cement floor. Fluorescent lights hanging from the twenty-four-foot high ceiling cast a cold glare. He noticed the only other door at the back of the cavernous room. Mykhailo took the seat next to the stranger at the eight-foot square metal table lost in the middle of the room. There were six more straight-back chairs and he wondered who would arrive.

The strangers looked at each other.

"I am Mykhailo Chernov."

"I am Pavio Kravets. Do you know why we are here?"

"No comrade, only that it was important and not an option."

They sat quietly, contemplating what was to come next.

The minutes dragged. The door opened. Six men entered the room. Two sat directly across from Mykhailo and Pavio with another two on either side. Pavio started tapping his fingers on the table. Mykhailo just looked straight ahead.

The man directly across from Mykhailo spoke first, "I am Ivan Kushnir, Pakhan (Godfather) of the Ukrainian Bratva (mafia brotherhood), and to my right is Vasili Petrov, Pakhan of the Russian Bratva. Joining us at the table are our Sovierniks (counsels) and Brigadiers (captains)."

Vasili continued, "We believe with the end of the cold war situation this would be a good time to expand our operations to another part of the world, specifically the United States. Great opportunities await someone who has the resources and strength to take advantage of the situation. Therefore, we have decided to combine our resources and add a new Bratva in the United States. Mykhailo, you have been my most trusted and competent Brigadier for many years, and I think it is time for you to move up in the family. You will be the new Pakhan in the United States."

A smile came across Mykhailo's face, "I am honored that you chose me, and I pledge my full support to you comrade. I can assure you I will bring honor to the Bratva."

Ivan broke in, "Pavio, you have been a loyal Boyevik (champion for a Brigadier), and we think it is time for you to move on. You will have your Brigade in the US, Bratva under Mykhailo, congratulations to you both."

Both Vasili and Ivan rose from their chairs and went to Mykhailo and Pavio. They put their hands on their shoulders and kissed them on both cheeks as a congratulatory sign.

A month later, Mykhailo moved his wife Lyresa and daughter Kira into a brownstone in the Brighton Beach section of Brooklyn, New York. He met with a Russian lawyer and started the groundwork for his new import business, Lyresa Imports.

Pavio would follow soon after.

With their connections in Russia and Ukraine, the business thrived, and soon Lyresa Imports was the largest importer of frozen crabs in the United States. Pavio handled underworld activities such as loan sharking and human sex trafficking.

Lyresa Imports had a contract with a handling company called General Warehousing (GW) located at New York's J.F. Kennedy Airport. To accommodate Lyresa's large frozen crab shipments, GW had to buy expensive refrigeration equipment for storage and transportation, adding a large amount of debt to the company. Mykhailo then threatened to move his operation elsewhere. GW had no alternative but to sell the company to Lyresa Imports. Mykhailo Chernov now had complete control of his import logistics. He renamed the warehouse Ground Services of America (GSA). Ivan Kushnir and Vasili Petrov became board members.

The operation grew with the addition of imports of oil equipment from Ukraine. Earthmoving equipment and toy helicopters from China came soon after.

CHAPTER THIRTEEN

Wednesday, 11:30 A.M.

Moshe entered the Bay House and saw Holly sitting at a table on the deck overlooking the bay. He was late. She was on time.

"Damn, that airport traffic. A fifteen-minute drive takes thirty minutes this time of day," explained Moshe.

"You don't have to tell me about traffic. I grew up on the world's largest parking lot, the Long Island Expressway," responded Holly.

There was a moment of silence as Moshe surveyed Holly's outfit. He focused on her red, open-front blouse. It was laced up the front but exposed most of her breasts. She was not wearing a bra.

"I know I asked you to dress seductively, but I didn't realize how tantalizing your breasts would be until this moment. Maybe we should forget this and get a hotel room."

"Not yet, first, we get the information. Then you can see what's up my skirt."

Moshe looked down at the tight black leather skirt with the slit in front, revealing most of her upper thigh.

"I can't wait. You look fabulous. I don't think anyone will be looking at anything but you today."

"Thanks."

Holly opened her purse, pulled out a tissue, and started wiping the droplets from her forehead.

Moshe reached out, and grabbed her hand.

"Your hands are clammy. Are you going to be OK? We can find another way."

She sat up. "No, I'll be fine," answered Holly, pulling back her hand and looking away.

"Sorry. I didn't mean to upset you."

Just then, Michelle, the bar manager, came to the table. "What can I get you guys?" she asked in a chirpy voice, a welcoming smile on her face.

"Sam Adams light," answered Holly.

"Same here."

"Two Sammy's coming up," said Michelle walking back to the bar.

"She's too cheery, and I'm not in a cheery mood."

"Don't let little things annoy you."

Michelle returned with their beers.

They were finishing their drinks when they spotted the huge aircraft fly over Jamaica Bay. It was time to leave for the cargo terminal.

"Let's get going," said Holly.

They arrived at the terminal just as the aircraft was taxiing towards the building.

Moshe took Holly into the building and escorted her past security into the warehouse. He left Holly to carry out her assignment.

Holly walked out of the building onto the back cargo ramp. Pavio was standing at the window watching the Antonov AN-124 pull up to the cargo terminal. He noticed Holly standing on the ramp, and rushed down the steps, two at a time, to the floor below and out the back door.

"Who are you? What are you doing out here? This is a restricted area," he demanded in a thick Ukrainian accent.

"Oh! I am so sorry. I just forgot where I was when I saw that beautiful plane. I'm with Moshe, and he told me not to leave the building. I apologize. I hope I didn't get Moshe in trouble. He was telling me about this operation last night at dinner and I was so fascinated, I had to see it."

"It's OK. Just come back here, into the building."

Pavio followed Holly back into the building. After calming down, he took note of her attributes. He decided to satisfy his suspicions by continuing the conversation.

"That is the Antonov AN124, one of the largest airplanes in the world," advised Pavio.

Holly asked, "What do you do here?"

"I am the Ukrainian Cargo Transport US representative. That's one of our aircraft. We have three others."

"All four arrive every day?"

"No! This one arrives here weekly. It starts in Kiev," continued Pavio, "which is our main base and takes heavy-duty earthmoving equipment and oil drilling supplies back and forth between Kiev and China. In China, it picks up small toy helicopters for our import company. Then it stops back in Kiev where it picks up more earth moving equipment."

"What exactly is earthmoving equipment?" asked Holly.

"Large bulldozers. They are used to clear vast areas for construction, usually superhighways. Sometimes we move excavating equipment used in strip mining. There is a storage facility in Kiev where we store equipment for the manufacturer in China. From there we transport it per their orders. It's cheaper for some companies just to lease the equipment for a project, rather than buy it."

"But don't you have to pay the US Custom duties? Wouldn't that be expensive and make the leasing unprofitable?"

"No. We import them under a carnet, so there is no duty to pay."

"What's a carnet?"

"A carnet is a passport for cargo. It allows you to bring in equipment temporarily as long as you send it back out within a specific time. Like when you have an orchestra traveling overseas. You can't have everyone paying duty for the same instrument in every country they perform in."

"They are huge," offered Holly trying to keep Pavio interested, as she watched one of the bulldozers drive down the aircraft's ramp.

"Normal cargo aircraft cannot carry these large machines."

"The next stop is here, at JFK Airport, where we unload the earth moving equipment. The toys are unloaded and stored in the warehouse until cleared by US Customs."

"What kind of toys?"

"Small nano quadcopters. Little helicopters that fit in the palm of your hand, which are flown by remote control. They are manufactured in China, and we are the sole importer in the United States."

Pavio continued, "The aircraft continues to Houston, where we deliver the oil pipes for oil rigs and pipelines before flying on to Stavanger, Norway.

"And you import oil pipes?"

"No! We just transport them between major oil drilling areas. They are too large to go on normal aircraft. Finally, we fly back to Kiev."

Suddenly, Pavio remembered he hadn't locked his office door. He noticed Moshe was not on the ramp. "Sorry, I must leave," he said to Holly, as he rushed toward the staircase.

While Holly was distracting Pavio, Moshe made his way up the stairs to Pavio's office. He looked around. With no one in sight, Moshe checked the handle; it was unlocked. By the window, he could see Pavio and Holly talking. He took a seat at Pavio's desk. There a security camera monitored the warehouse. Moshe saw Pavio escort, Holly, back into the warehouse. They were watching the unloading. The computer was open on the desk. Pavio, in his rush, had failed to sign off. A quick scan of the files revealed one labeled, *Bee Hives*. Moshe started reading. It described a scheme to sell the altered drones to ISIS in the United States. *Just what I need.* He pulled a flash drive from his pocket and started to copy the file. But he quickly noticed Pavio was no longer with Holly. It was time to leave. He checked the screen. Almost finished. Finally, he removed the flash drive. Moshe rushed out of the office and down the back stairs. He jumped on a forklift and headed for the aircraft.

After opening the door of his office, Pavio checked his computer, all looked fine. He scanned the ramp just as Moshe was pulling one of the ULDs, containing the toy helicopters, from the aircraft. *I'm becoming paranoid about this operation,* thought Pavio.

Moshe drove by Holly. He stepped off the forklift and kissed Holly goodbye while slipping something into her purse.

"I'll meet you at your house after my shift."

Holly turned but bumped into Alexi as she was leaving. He gave her a hard look but did not say anything. The chill came back.

It was after 3 p.m. when she left the airport. The rush hour traffic was horrendous. Stop and go traffic continued from the Belt Parkway and through the Long Island Expressway. Holly did not arrive at her home in Port Jefferson until after six. After entering the empty house, she poured herself a Knob Creek, no ice. She took a sip. Her hands were sweating and shaking. The ringtone from her cell phone echoed throughout the house.

"Hi, Holly. It's Cas."

"What did you find out?"

"Nothing."

"Nothing? What do you mean?"

"The guy doesn't exist. No social media, no Facebook, no Twitter, nothing. I couldn't find a credit score, no credit cards, no phone listing. He doesn't even have a driver's license or owns a car. I think you should dump this guy now. You may like this guy, but he scares the shit out of me."

"Me too, but it's too late. I just helped him get some information we were looking for at Ground Services. He's coming tonight. I'm certain he has information that will help Jeff."

"Just be careful."

"I will."

The front door slammed. John yelled out, "Holly, we're home."

Holly hung up.

CHAPTER FOURTEEN

Port Jefferson, 6:30 P.M.

Holly leaped out of her chair as Moshe entered the room. "What did you find out?"

"First, how's Jeff?"

"Doing great. He'll be home Friday, but will still need some home care," she responded.

"Holly, where's your handbag?"

"On the table," said Holly pointing towards the dining room.

Moshe fished through the side pocket and pulled out the flash drive.

"How did this get here?" Holly frowned.

"I dropped it in your bag when I kissed you goodbye."

"And here, I thought that was a kiss of affection."

"It was, but I had to hide the drive from Pavio. He was watching me from the window. Now, are you going to get me a PC, or are we going to look at this stupid thing the rest of the night?"

"OK, I'm going. Hold your water."

"What?"

"Never mind, it's an old saying. Give me a second," said Holly as she ran to her bedroom.

"Did you get what you were looking for?" John asked.

"We'll know soon," answered Moshe.

Holly retrieved a laptop from her room, and Moshe inserted the flash drive. John and Holly looked over his shoulder. They stared at the screen. *Операция Пульсар,Частный, суббота,1:00 вечера.* The unreadable script went on for many pages. On and on…

"It's useless. The drive must have been faulty. All that work for nothing. Gibberish," cried John as he turned to Pat.

Sitting on the sofa, Pat remarked, "All that for nothing." She took out a tissue to wipe her eyes.

Moshe continued to scroll down frantically, still looking.

"It looks like Russian," said Holly. "Can you translate it, Moshe?"

"Yes, but I need a pen and paper to write this down. Could I get a cup of coffee? This is going to take some time."

John handed Moshe a yellow legal pad and pen from his desk drawer while Pat prepared a pot of coffee. The night progressed slowly. Holly paced behind Moshe's shoulder, trying to read his notes. They made no sense to her.

Finally, Moshe got up and paced around the room. He was shaking his head. Lines appeared on his forehead. His lips were locked tightly.

"What is it?" inquired a concerned Holly.

"It is worse than we thought. This is bad, awful."

Once again, the family's faces dropped.

"No! It's OK... for Jeff. I believe I found out why they murdered Stepan," explained Moshe.

"Then, why so bad?" Holly asked a question Moshe had refused to answer.

"What I found is so dangerous that if you knew, your lives would be in danger just as Stepan's was. I can't and won't do that. I need to make a private call."

Moshe pulled a cellphone from his pocket and dialed a number. He started speaking in Russian as he walked from the room. A few minutes later, he returned.

Holly took Moshe into the kitchen.

"What's going on?" Holly sternly demanded, "You're not going to leave me out now, after what I did today."

"OK, I have some friends in international law enforcement, who I just called with the information. They will be contacting the various agencies needed to deal with this crisis. I am waiting for a callback, confirming what they have done. Can I have a drink of vodka? Russian, if you have it."

Holly opened the refrigerator, "We have a bottle of Stolichnaya."

"Close enough. No ice."

They joined John and Pat in the living room. Just then, Moshe's cell phone chirped. He read the text message.

"OK, everything is being arranged. We have a meeting with the DA tomorrow morning," announced Moshe.

"All of us?" John inquired.

"No, just Holly and me. You and Pat are out of it."

"Why don't you stay here tonight?" suggested Holly.

"We'd be honored to have you as our guest after all you've done for us," assured Pat.

"Thank you for your generous offer, but I have some things to complete at my apartment."

With that, Holly escorted Moshe to his car.

"You have done so much for us. How can I repay you?" asked Holly.

"You already have," answered Moshe. He looked into her green eyes and stroked her hair. Their lips touched. Their tongues crossed.

She pulled away, "You should stay."

"There's still lots to do. I'll meet you at the DA's office," said Moshe as he left.

Holly went into the house and asked, "Where's dad?"

"He was exhausted and went to bed," answered Pat. "Are you all right? You look like something is troubling you."

"There is."

"Can I help?"

"Mom, did you have any regrets about getting married?"

"Why would you ask such a stupid question? Your father was the best thing that ever happened to me."

"I meant about not having your own career. You have a degree. You could have achieved so much."

"I did. I had you and Jeff. No regrets whatsoever."

"Yes. But do you ever think you should have waited before getting married?"

"Never. I think something is bothering you. Moshe, perhaps?"

"Does it show?"

"Very much."

"Something is intoxicating about Moshe. I'm not certain… what it is. Perhaps it's the feeling of mystery. I can't help myself."

"Look, we all have to make decisions in our lives, some good and some bad. Even the bad ones can turn around if you work at it."

"How?" Holly asked.

"I don't think I ever told you, but when I first met your father, we were both in college. I was going to Hofstra University and he was at Saint Louis University in Missouri. After a few months, I found someone else and sent him a *Dear John* letter. I regretted it shortly after. The new beau was an asshole. But you know what happened?"

"No, stop stalling. What happened?"

"Well, a few years after graduation, I was on a date at Palisades Park. It was an amusement park in New Jersey of all places. They're condos now. But, there I was on the Ferris wheel with my date and who do I spot in the crowd below."

"Father."

"Correct. He was on a blind date. There was another couple, and I recognized the other guy, Bobby. I called out his name and he waved. When I got off the ride, they were waiting for me. We were dating the following week."

"Wow! You never told me that one."

"So, it may still work out for you."

At his apartment, Moshe lay in bed, going over what he would say at tomorrow's meeting. He hoped they would understand the severity of the threat.

The building shook. A bomb went off. A soldier had fallen beside Moshe, still breathing. Moshe's ears were ringing, and he could not hear anything. The building was about to collapse. Moshe picked up the soldier and placed him on his back. He carried him out of the building fireman style. Shots were whizzing past him but Moshe couldn't hear them, only see where they hit the road and building. He ran to the building across the street and found a safe spot under a staircase. Crouching down, Moshe wrapped his arms around his fallen comrade and pointed his Uzi toward the door. He was prepared to shoot a friend or foe attempting to enter the building. What seemed like hours was only minutes when his hearing returned. It would be a full hour before a rescue team appeared. But it was too late for his fallen soldier.

Moshe woke up to a soaking-wet bed. He got up and pulled the sheets off and headed for the washing machine. Moshe dropped the sheets and his wet shorts into the machine. He continued back into the bedroom to his adjoining bathroom, where he stepped into the shower. The cold water, from the rain shower head, gave relief to his night terrors. As he stayed and enjoyed the calming moment, he realized he had not had this recurring dream for at least a year. The pressure of the assignment had brought it back. Back in Jalula, Iraq that fateful night, he was lying in urine while waiting for the rescue. That had been June 8, 2014, the scariest day of his life. Moshe had felt vulnerable without his senses. He would always fear going blind or deaf from then on.

Finally, he exited the shower and dried himself off. He entered the bedroom and walked up to his dresser and pulled a pair of black boxer shorts from the drawer.

He marched into the living room and picked up a crystal tumbler from the bar. Continuing into the kitchen, he placed the glass under the icemaker on the refrigerator door. The ice clinked into the glass. He turned and leaned against the door. He put the glass on his forehead and rolled it back and forth, relishing the coolness. Finally he opened the door of the refrigerator and pulled out a cold bottle of ZYR. He poured three fingers of the Russian vodka into the glass and took a long sip.

CHAPTER FIFTEEN

One Year Earlier in Southwestern Syria

Russian Special Forces (Spetsnaz GRU), led by General Dimitri Kuznetsov, were preparing to test a new weapon on the Joban neighborhood of Damascus, Syria. The city lay on a plateau sheltered by the Anti-Lebanon Mountains. A contract was awarded to three high tech companies to develop a weapon to protect Russian soldiers during house to house fighting in the populated cities. Today, Kharkiv Technical Center (KTC) was preparing to demonstrate an autonomous weapon system designed by their research facility in Kiev.

For a week, the Syrian troops had attempted to remove the last of the Syrian rebels to no avail. Syrian artillery shelled the city for twenty-four hours, but still, the resistance was intense. The Syrian soldiers hesitated to reenter the city. General Kuznetsov ordered all military personnel to leave the city. He then called for Syrian Air Force helicopters to drop barrel bombs, consisting of high explosives, shrapnel and oil. The town was leveled. Rubble was all that was left of the buildings. The inferno badly burned any civilians who were not killed immediately. Black smoke blocked out the sun during the day and the continuing fires lit the sky at night.

General Kuznetsov called to his orderly, "Bring me the Kharkiv representatives."

Illya Fedorov walked up, "You asked for me, General?"

"Yes, the fires are finally out, and it is now cool enough to enter the city. My men tell me there are still many rebel snipers hiding in the rubble. Now explain to me what I am about to witness."

"We will be deploying a number of carrier helicopters over the city. The carriers contain smaller helicopters we call bees. Once in position, we will activate the carriers, which will then release the bees. The bees will swarm into the city and attack the rebels."

"How exactly are these bees, as you call them, going to help me?"

"Well, they contain a small number of explosives, and when the bees come in contact with anything, they explode," advised Illya.

"That little explosive device will kill a man?"

"Yes, if it is detonated in the right spot, like the head."

"So it must hit the head to be effective. I don't see how that will help my men."

"When the bees attack, the enemy will try to swat them away, like a fly. But as soon as a hand hits one, it will be blown off. He will be incapacitated. People will attempt to help only to get attacked themselves. Fear will disrupt your enemy's will to fight."

"How do they know who to attack?" questioned the General.

"They have recognition technology which will identify humans."

"What about civilians?"

"I'm afraid they will be considered collateral damage."

"And my men? Do you consider them collateral damage," demanded Kuznetsov.

"Oh no! General. We distributed insignia patches to your men that the bees will recognize as friendlies."

"Artem, come here," called out Illya to his assistant.

"Yes, Illya. What do you need?"

"Are we ready to proceed?" asked the General.

"Yes, General, we have set the devices and are prepared for the test. When your men surround the city, we will release two hundred nano-helicopters. They have localization technology and custom body recognition algorithms to detect and differentiate humans from any other species, such as sand cats. They also can enter buildings through windows as well as doors. They can even be programmed to explode windows, allowing other drones to enter and search out enemies."

"My men are in place, but what will happen to them?" questioned General Kuznetsov.

"Nothing. The patches we discussed will protect your men," answered the KTC representative.

"OK, let's begin," Kuznetsov ordered the drones into the city while his forces waited outside.

A few minutes later, the KTC technicians released the drones. Immediately, the drones began to seek out their targets. As they struck, the enemy attempted to shoot down the drones. But because they were equipped with sophisticated circuitry and three Piego electric gyros, they were extremely maneuverable. The drones targeted the enemy's exposed skin, particularly the face and neck area. That was their kill zone. Death came almost instantly. The rebels tried swatting them like bugs, but this only caused the drones to explode and blow off fingers and hands. As the insurgents attempted to escape the onslaught, some ran into doorways, followed by the drones. The result was the same, death, or only to reappear with blood gushing from their wounds, and be finished off by other drones. The drones did not discriminate. They also targeted women and children. All was going as planned until General Kuznetsov's men entered the city. Suddenly the drones turned and started attacking the General's men. They tried to fight back with the same results as the enemy. Blood was everywhere. Men were running, trying to hide from the drones. The drones pursued the General's staff. It was only by a miracle that the General was able to take cover inside a nearby tank. Not all of his team were so lucky. Two of his officers died and many more were wounded.

Finally, after what seemed like hours, the drones were disabled by the KTC team, but not until five more Russian soldiers died. The General was furious and called for the KTC team. In front of all his men, he screamed at the KTC representative.

"Two of my best officers died today. Eight soldiers killed, many more wounded. I would have had fewer casualties without your help. You fucking killed my men," yelled the red-faced General. His hands were shaking.

After a few minutes of listening to the General's ranting, the KTC representative started to explain, "Perhaps your men should not have covered the patches which identified them as friendlies?" Immediately, the General pulled out his Grach pistol, yelled "fuck you," and shot the representative in the forehead. Before the other KTC representative could say anything, Kuznetsov struck him across the face with his pistol. "You say a fucking word, and you will join your piece of shit friend. Now get him out of my sight and go."

The contract with KTC was immediately canceled, and the other members of the team ran back to Kiev in disgrace.

Once back in Kiev, the remaining representatives had to explain what had happened. There they waited in the KTC boardroom. The KTC Board of Directors, including Mykhailo Chernov, Vasili Petrov, Ivan Kushnir, and Vladyslav Kolisnyk, President of Kharkiv Technical Center, entered through the large oak doors. KTC's three remaining representatives were shaking, looking down at the ground. The President ordered, "Which of you is going to explain what occurred?"

"I guess I will. I was standing next to Illya as he got shot," answered the representative with the swollen face.

"What is your name?" Vlad snapped.

"I am Artem Bakaj, assistant sales manager."

"Explain how this disaster occurred and how one of my valued employees died."

He explained. "We had given the Russians the identity devices which would identify them as friendlies. The drones would not attack anyone with the device. The problem was some of the men had covered the identifiers with their equipment."

"What kind of equipment?"

"Their shoulder straps for their rifles for one thing. Some had protective vests on that covered the safety devices. We did not take into consideration that the identifiers would not be visible or we would have had them equipped to send out a signal to the drones."

"Can't we do that now?" Vlad continued the interrogation.

"No. The drones are not equipped to receive a signal, only to identify by sight."

"What did the General say to this?"

"The General was emphatic that there would be no more funds and did not want to hear from us again. When Illya tried to suggest that the General's men should not have covered the identifiers, the General shot him in the head."

Vlad ordered the representatives out of the room,

After some discussion, Vlad was asked, "How much money did KTC invest in the project?" He offered, "We are in for 84,471,000 Ukrainian hryvnias or three million US dollars."

"That is more than I am willing to accept," stated Ivan Kushnir.

Mykhailo Chernov stood up. "I think I have a way to recoup or at least minimize our losses, comrades."

"How?"

"I suggest we offer this weapon to the highest bidder. We can contact some of the terrorist groups."

"Which ones?"

"There are bands of the Islamic State in hiding. Also, I believe there is still a branch of Al Qaeda underground. I also believe the Taliban might be interested or perhaps Hamas."

"I believe you have given us an answer to our problem. How many of these drones do we have on hand?"

"I estimate there are just under three thousand of the small drones and one hundred of the carriers," answered Vlad.

"I know of an arms dealer who has done business in the past with these groups. Let me have him negotiate with them for us," said Mykhailo.

"OK. Keep us informed," said Vlad as he ended the meeting.

Mykhailo met with Ivan Kushnir and Vasili Petrov a few months later.

"What is the status of your negotiations, Mykhailo?" Vasili asked.

"Well, my contact talked with the Taliban and Al Qaeda, both showed no interest. Hamas wanted them for long-range, but they felt the two-mile maximum range for the drones would not get them over the border into Israel."

"So we failed?" questioned Ivan.

"No. We had talks with ISIS, and they are interested and have the funds we require."

"Where did you have this meeting?"

"I don't know where the actual meetings transpired. It was a secret camp. I think one was in Afghanistan. I used a secured satellite cell phone given me. The phone conferenced me into the meeting."

"OK. How will that work?"

"We told them, 'we are sure General Kuznetsov would have used these against the Islamic State eventually. Why not turn the tables against him? That piqued their interest."

"How?"

"They were not interested in Kuznetsov, but interested in the United States. They want them delivered into the United States. I told them no problem. We could deliver to JFK in New York. That impressed them."

"Why?"

"ISIS has independent cells located throughout the world. The ones in Syria and Afghanistan were not receptive. But there is one in the US, and they are the ones who took the offer."

"How will they use them in the US?"

"They would not tell me. But they want them in hand no later than 25 September."

"Why then?"

"One of Pavio's drug dealers has a customer whose brother is connected to ISIS. They told him to leave the city no later than September 30."

"What's September 30?"

"Nothing but on October 1 the Jets will be playing at home in the Giants stadium and t,he Yankee's have a home game on the same day. I think they want to strike both venues on the same day."

"OK! Let's do it."

.

CHAPTER SIXTEEN

Thursday, Suffolk County District Attorney's Office

Moshe and Holly entered the H. Lee Dennison Building at 100 Veterans Memorial Highway in Hauppauge, Long Island, New York at 9:30 a.m.

Moshe approached the police officer stationed at the screening entrance, "We're here to see Susan Shepard."

"The DA's office is on the third floor. Place all items on the belt and proceed through the scanner," responded the officer.

Holly placed her pocketbook on the belt and watched as it passed through the x-ray machine. Moshe emptied his pockets into the small tray and put it on the belt. A quick walk through the body scanner and they were on their way to the nearby elevator.

A secretary greeted them as they enter Susan Shepard's office.

"How can I help you?" she asked.

"We have a meeting with the District Attorney this morning. My name is Moshe Kaplan, and this is Holly Flynn."

"Yes. They are expecting you. Please come this way." She opened the door to a room of people gathered around a large table.

"What's this all about? I don't have all day," said Mike York to the group.

"Oh! Here they are now," said Susan Shepard. The tall, slender brunette, dressed in a charcoal suit with a white dress shirt opened at the collar, set her coffee aside and rose from her chair. "Good Morning, Miss Flynn. How is your brother doing?"

"Much better now. Thank you for asking."

"And the infamous, Mr. Kaplan, I believe," as she offered her hand to Moshe.

Holly had an astonished look on her face

"Would you care for some coffee?" continued Susan.

"No, thanks."

"Then why don't you take these seats beside me?"

Moshe thanked her for meeting with them.

"Before we begin, I would like everyone to introduce themselves? I'll start. Susan Shepard, Suffolk County District Attorney."

"Captain Michael York, NYPD Emergency Service Unit (ESU)."

"Captain Sam Shapiro, NYPD Intelligence Officer, Hercules counterterrorism bureau."

"John Stevenson, Homeland Security," said Stevenson as he used his right hand to keep his left hand from shaking.

"Special Agent Steven Johnson, Federal Bureau of Investigation."

"Detective Chief Superintendent Anna Sokolov, Interpol."

"Moshe Kaplan, Diplomatic Attaché, attached to the Israeli Embassy, in NYC."

Holly's eyes opened wide, and her jaw dropped as she turned her head to Moshe and whispered, "What the hell is this? You have some explaining to do Mister."

"OK! I'll tell you everything later," he whispered back.

"Holly Flynn, my brother is charged with the murder of his friend Stepan. We believe it was carried out by this group."

"Thank you all. Now, Mr. Kaplan, can you please explain what is going on, now that we have all parties assembled."

"Yes. Thank you. First, here is the flash drive I copied from Pavio Kravets' computer at the GSA cargo terminal. This has all the information, but it is in Russian. I have a handout that explains in English, what is about to transpire."

Moshe handed out the sheets which detailed two Russian and Ukrainian Mafia families, linked together through a robotics research and development company named Kharkiv Technical Center or KTC located in Kiev. Mykhailo Chernov ran a third mafia family established in New York through his JFK importing and cargo handling companies.

"So, where are we going with this information?" questioned a skeptical Capt. York as he held up his glasses in his hand.

"Several months ago, we received information from reliable sources, indicating that certain sophisticated weapons were offered to our neighbors specifically, Hamas in Palestine. My government tasked me with infiltrating Chernov's cargo handling company, Ground Services America or GSA. Since working undercover at GSA, I found that Hamas was not willing to pay the price, and the weapons are now coming here to the US."

"What weapons and to whom?" York continued as he leaned back in his chair.

"LAWs and ISIS," Moshe replied.

"I know who ISIS is, but the only laws I know are on the books," a confused Shepard confessed.

"LAWs, Lethal Autonomous Weapons systems are miniature remote drones that can cause death and destruction. In this case, we are talking about nano quadcopters capable of killing people. We found a surveillance video on a dead Syrian rebel's body camera. It showed the drones attacking rebels or what was left of them."

Moshe walked over to the computer and inserted the video into the drive. The nano quadcopter appeared on the screen. It was only slightly bigger than a quarter. "Of course, this is not the actual one, but you can see how small it is." He paused the video.

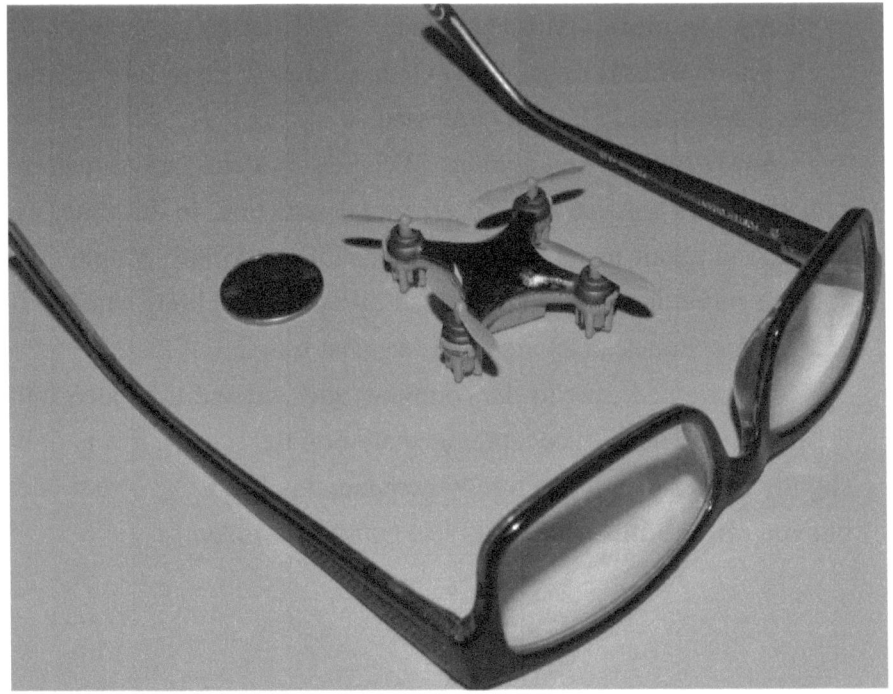

"The damn thing looks harmless to me." York was skeptical once again.

"Let me give you an example. These tiny toys contain a small number of explosives, enough to possibly blow out someone's brains, a leg, or an arm. If you'd like, I can continue the video but I must warn you it is very graphic."

"No need at this time. Please continue, Moshe," said Shepard.

"Sure. Now, send a thousand of these small toys to an event, such as a football game, and have them attack the fans. You have hysterical people running for their lives. You now have a terrorist attack. ISIS doesn't care if they kill or maim as long as there is terror involved."

"OK, fine," York removed his glasses for emphasis and asked, "But how do they get these toys to attack someone?"

"This is where Kharkiv Tech came into the picture. They had a contract with the Russian government to develop robots that would attack their enemies in the field. But the contract was canceled when they found there were target identification issues. The drones started attacking everyone."

"Alright, so now we have a toy that attacks everyone," confirmed York.

"Well, kind of. It has a sophisticated circuitry that has human body recognition technology. It identifies humans. The same technology is used in photography to remove a person from one scene and insert them into another. By sending them into an event remotely, the terrorists are out of harm's way. They have developed larger remote-control helicopters, called hives, that can carry up to two dozen small ones called bees up to a mile away. Using onboard cameras, they can fly to the event and release the nano quadcopters. Ten hives can release 240 bees called a swarm and attack everyone in their vicinity."

"How many are we talking about?" questioned Johnson.

"Thousands. Maybe more."

"How do they plan to gain entry into the country, undetected?" asked Stevenson as he tossed his glasses on the table and stared at Moshe.

"Toys! They have been coming into the country for the last three years as toys. They would be treated just like any other harmless toys coming in every week. Customs review would not find any difference from prior shipments. There will be four aircraft pallets on board the AN124 this Saturday, arriving from Kiev. Three pallets will have the quadcopters, and one will have the hives. Three thousand total bees and one hundred beehives."

"This sounds like science fiction to me. Just another story. I never heard of it, and I fly all the time." Susan Shepard continued, "What does this AN124 look like?"

"An Antonov AN124 is one of the largest cargo aircraft in the world. It does not carry passengers, only cargo, and usually extremely large cargo like other airplanes and engines. The Russians developed it to transport troops and equipment to isolated locations where they did not have the equipment to remove the load in the usual way. The aircraft actually 'kneels' down, and a ramp extends from the front and the back to allow tanks and other equipment to drive on board."

"Sam, what do you have to say?" asked Shepard.

"We've seen an increase in chatter regarding some kind of operation but have not been able to pinpoint what it is or where it will occur, let alone when. But, this sounds like the type of action ISIS would love. Terrorists know the benefit of sensational media coverage."

"We need to devise a three-part plan. First, find the source, intercept the shipment, and capture the bastards," said York.

"Is everyone in agreement?" asked Shepard.

The room was quiet. Everyone was scanning their IPads and Notebooks. Some had their hands on the side of their heads, and others just stared at the table.

Finally, Mike offered, "I can set up my SWAT team at the airport to intercept the shipment when it arrives at JFK."

Moshe interrupted, "I'm sorry to break in, Captain York, but can you tell me more about your SWAT team?"

"Sure," Captain York responded. "the NYPD Emergency Service Unit (ESU) is a regular manned component of the police department, as opposed to the SWAT collateral duty function found in most law enforcement agencies. When one is assigned to ESU, that is their full-time duty station until they move on. They don't work patrol, don't become detectives, or have any other assignment when not performing ESU functions. ESU has its own chain of command, and is integrated into the NYPD in the same way that patrol precincts and other NYPD functions are." York continued, "all ESU members receive training in heavy weapons and tactics, operating explosive removal vehicles, SCUBA, EMT, high angle rescue, vehicle, and train extrication, in addition to HazMat Level 1, suicide prevention/mediation, and dignitary protection. We support the community in many ways."

Johnson added, "I can support York. I will get some of my people in positions in aircraft maintenance and refueling. That will give us people at the aircraft when it pulls up to the cargo facility."

"Anna, is everything all right?" asked Shepard.

"Yes, I was just cleaning off a spot on my teaspoon." She continued, "Interpol already has people in position at Boryspil International Airport, at the cargo terminal, maintenance building and fueling station. We could take down the operation today, but we want to get those people in the United States also. You must play by the rules here, so I understand it is not so easy."

"So how do we know if the shipment is on the way?" York inquired.

"Our people in Kiev will be watching the loading of the aircraft at Boryspil. As soon as they can confirm, it is loaded and takes off," said Sokolov looking straight at Moshe, "you will be advised."

"OK. I'll station my SWAT off Rockaway Boulevard. From there, we can see the aircraft approaching and landing. We can be on-site in less than ten minutes. Plenty of time to be at the cargo facility when the aircraft approaches," said York.

"Is everyone in agreement?" Shepard requested a consensus.

"Yes," said York.

"I'm good," answered Johnson.

"How about you, Anna?" asked Shepard, looking directly at her.

"I have been ready for over a year."

"We need a name for this operation," said Shepard.

York stood and suggested, "How about Operation Red Rover?"

"Because of drones?"

"No. Remember the game you played as a child? Red Rover, Red Rover, send someone over. You had two teams, and one team would lock arms and the other would send one of their players over to break the other team's line."

"Yeah, we're sending Moshe to break up the terrorists," said Johnston.

"OK, then. Everyone agreed? Operation Red Rover it is. Now get your teams together and call me as soon as you're ready. I will coordinate with the rest of the group. Good luck, and keep your people safe." Shepard rose from the table and headed towards the door.

"Wait!" yelled out Stevenson.

Everyone stopped and turned toward the man from Homeland Security.

"What is it, John?"

"You've left out DHS. I feel slighted." Stevenson's left hand was shaking badly.

"You are right. This is DHS's operation. I just arranged the meeting at the request of Mr. Kaplan. Everyone will coordinate through John. DHS will track the entire operation."

The others shook hands and said their goodbyes.

Susan Shepard thanked everyone for coming as they left.

CHAPTER SEVENTEEN

Thursday, New York 11:00 a.m.

Anna Sokolov went back to her hotel, a bare-bones Super 6. She placed the paper bag with the Dunkin Donuts coffee and an apple fritter on the small desk in the corner, using a sanitary wipe from her purse to disinfect the top. She went into the bathroom and washed her hands in the sink for the third time in the last hour. The faucet continued to drip. The cracked light switch plate cracked the exposed wires. She made sure her hands were extra dry before switching off the light. Anna wore her socks to bed so her bare feet would not touch the worn and torn carpet. *New York is an expensive city. I wish Interpol would increase the per diem.*

Finally, it was time to call her contact in Kiev. She punched in the number on her encrypted satellite phone. After two rings, someone answered.

"Illya, it is Anna. How was your day?"

"Strange, Petrov was here visiting Kushnir. They were in a closed meeting all day. I could not hear what they were talking about."

"Do you think there is a change for Saturday morning?"

"No, everything is the same. The flight is planned to leave here, in Kiev, at 7 a.m. on Saturday and should arrive in New York by noon."

"Good. How is your wife?"

"She is fine but wants me to quit. She thinks it is getting too dangerous."

"You can't quit now. We are getting close."

"I know. But this is the last one. After this is completed, I'm turning n my papers."

"You are going to retire? Can you afford it?"

"I think so. Perhaps I can get some small private assignments to supplement my income."

"Well, good luck. I will help you any way I can."

"Thank you. How was your meeting with the New York City Police?" Illya continued. "I hear they can be difficult to work with."

"Perhaps, but all I have to do is tell them when the aircraft departs, confirming the helicopters are on board. NYPD and the FBI will do the rest."

"What about the ISIS cell in the US? Aren't they going to arrest them?"

"Ms. Shepard, the DA, felt they would not have a case unless they let the ISIS cell take possession of the drones and attempt a terrorist act with them. The man from Homeland Security felt they would get enough information from the raid to identify the cell. But rather than arrest them, he would track them to other cells. The important thing was to confiscate and destroy the drones before they could do any harm."

"Those rules again," Illya shook his head as he said it. "I will call you personally as soon as the aircraft is in flight."

"Thank you. What is your plan?" Anna asked.

"Your operation starts during our p.m. shift here in Kiev. I have all my men working that shift. As soon as you confirm you have the drones, we will make our arrests."

"I will call you when we have the shipment. Then you can arrest them all."

"I heard them talking about meeting here before the big celebration dinner party that night. I guess I will arrest them then," advised Illya.

"That would be great if you could catch them all in one place. Perhaps you could take pictures of their faces with your camera. I would love to see their reaction," Anna said, unable to keep from laughing.

"I think I can do that." Illya boasted.

"Thanks. Call me on Saturday as soon as you have the confirmation."

"I will. Good night."

"It's not night here, and I just had breakfast. Good night, Illya."

She disconnected.

2:00 p.m. New York Time

Moshe and Holly were back in Holly's car, driving to Port Jefferson.

"Damn traffic," mumbled Holly. "What happens now?"

"Nothing for us. We just wait. I'm going back to work, I had to switch with one of the other guys to get this morning off."

"OK. I think I'll just stay with Mom and Dad at Jeff's bedside. Sam Baum called this morning. The police are no longer interested in him, at least for now."

"Great, then you'll be taking him home tomorrow."

"Oh, yes! First thing," answered Holly with a grin.

They arrived at Holly's, and Moshe kissed her and left.

"Call me," yelled Holly as Moshe was leaving.

"I will, in the morning. First thing," Moshe yelled back, smiling.

CHAPTER EIGHTEEN

Friday, 9:00 a.m. Briefing. SWAT Headquarters Lower Manhattan

Gentlemen, was a term Captain Mike York used infrequently, but he used it today. "Gentlemen," Captain Mike York began. Everyone in the room chuckled.

"JFK is performing an emergency drill tomorrow at 1 P.M. They have asked us to participate in a hostage situation with a Boeing 777 aircraft, which will take place at the end of taxiway 4L."

Mike did not want anyone to know what was going on before tomorrow. The Russian Mafia had long ears.

"Do we just show up at 1 p.m.?" questioned one of the officers.

"No, we'll meet at the JFK Postal Facility. Let's see, ah, 11 a.m."

"Man, there goes my lunch break," a disgruntled officer remarked.

"Have a larger breakfast. Besides, I think you owe me some hours, for those long breaks you've been taking the last couple of weeks."

They all laughed.

"OK, be safe," Mike ordered as he was leaving.

Friday, 11:00 a.m., Stony Brook Hospital.

Holly arrived at Jeff's room and gave him a hello kiss. Pat and John were seated next to Jeff's bed.

"Did you bring my clothes?"

"In the bag," replied Holly handing Jeff the grey sports bag.

"Thanks."

Pat said, "The doctor just left and said he's free to go. Is that true, Holly?"

"Well, kinda," Holly summed up the situation: "The DA has put your case on hold pending tomorrow's airport operation. Meanwhile, you are free on your own recognizance."

Jeff asked his mother and Holly to leave while he dressed.

The nurse entered with a wheelchair.

"I'm good," advised Jeff.

"Sorry. Orders. No one leaves on his own."

Reluctantly, Jeff slid into the wheelchair.

"I'll get the car and bring it up front," Holly announced.

Meanwhile, the nurse wheeled Jeff and his entourage to the front of the building, where Holly was waiting. After her family was safely in the car, she proceeded to Port Jefferson.

Friday, 1:00 p.m., FBI Headquarters, 26 Federal Plaza, New York

Steve Johnson was meeting with his undercover agents in his windowless office, located in the middle of the twenty-third floor. Surrounding his office were the agent cubicles, twenty-five in all. The half walls were aluminum panels covered in beige vinyl. Fluorescent lighting shined down on the white vinyl speckled flooring. Each cubicle contained a desk with a laptop computer and a chair. Personal items identified each employee's area. Fred Willard and Thomas Payne left their cubicles and entered Steve Johnson's office.

Johnson closed the blinds for privacy and went over the plan and what was expected from the police SWAT team, as well as Fred and Tom's roles in the operation.

"Thomas, you're the mechanic from Triangle Maintenance, and Fred, you're the fueler from Allied Fueling," Steve Johnson continued, "Are we set?"

"We're ready," Fred assured Steve.

"One more thing. An undercover agent is working at GSA. His name is Moshe Kaplan. He's 6 foot 3 inches tall, about 210 pounds, and very muscular, with short, curly black hair. He'll be wearing a GSA warehouse uniform but will have an FBI identification tag hanging around his neck once the action starts. Please, don't shoot him. I don't want one of you bozo's killing the guy. No friendly fire shit. Here me?"

"Aw, you don't let us have any fun," said Tom with a smirk on his face.

"Laugh all you want. But it'll be your ass on the hot seat, not mine."

"We'll try not to, but no guarantees," Fred answered with a hearty laugh.

"OK, see you tomorrow. I'll let you know if anything changes."

Friday, 6:00 p,m, local time, Kiev

Ivan Kushnir and Vasili Petrov met at the Ground Services Ukraine (GSU) office. The room was sparse, with grey cinderblock walls and a concrete floor. The only furniture consisted of a metal filing cabinet, a wooden desk and three chairs. They went over the plans for Saturday morning's scenario. After a year of negotiations, they had a buyer willing to pay the $10,000,000 that Ivan and Vasili had demanded. Their plan to transport the merchandise into the United States was meticulously worked out.

"Ivan, once more, comrade. How is the money being transferred?" Vasili wanted to ensure he got his share.

"Once the ISIS cell takes possession of the merchandise at JFK, they will wire transfer the funds to our bank in Switzerland. There, they have instructions to split the sum equally into three parts. Each part will be wired to each of our accounts, yours, mine and Mykhailo's simultaneously," Ivan continued, "The complete process should take no more than ten minutes."

"How do we know they will not leave before the money is transferred?" Inquired Vasili, wringing his hands.

"Mykhailo Chernov has given orders that the merchandise will not leave his dock until the money transfer is completed."

"You are satisfied with the plan?" Vasili needed to be assured once again.

"*Yabat-kapat*, you act like a *babushka.*" Ivan threw his hands in the air. "I have it under control. It is all arranged. The aircraft will come around the building and pull up to the back apron.[4] There, we will proceed with the loading. Once everything is on board, the aircraft takes off. All we have to do is wait for our money."

"I am satisfied. Then we can have a nice bowl of borscht and varenyky, yes?" suggested Vasili.

"Yes, Vasili. And vodka comrade, plenty of vodka."

---

[4] A part of the airport field for plane parking, loading and unloading passengers, luggage and cargo.

CHAPTER NINETEEN

Saturday, 4:00 a.m. Local Time Kiev, GSU Warehouse

I llya Kozlov galumphed into the GSU warehouse for his 4 a.m. shift. His six-foot frame struggled to carry his 275-pound body. A potbelly from too much vodka and borscht hung over his belt. Black, close-cropped hair sat atop his round face which was covered by stubble. A red bulbous nose with puss-filled bumps sat above his puffy lips. Bloodshot eyes gave away a sleepless night. Black ink tattoos covered his arms, back, chest and shoulders moving up onto his thick neck. He was wearing an ushanka (a fur cap with ear flaps) and orange coveralls with GSU in large letters across his back.

"Illya," called out the GSU supervisor, "go out back and clear the apron for this morning's flight."

"Which aircraft, comrade supervisor?" Illya answered.

"Flight YT450, aircraft registration identifier **URKRN**, estimated time of arrival is now 04:45 hours."

"*Da*, immediately," Illya answered as he continued trudging to the back apron. He lined up the dollies[5] on the side of the ramp out of the way of the incoming aircraft. Any debris was removed from the ground so as not to be ingested into the engines. Forklifts were parked next to the building. Tug tow vehicles were parked by the dollies.

The sixty-five thousand square meter warehouse was the height of a five-story building. Offices occupied the front half of the second floor with the back half of the building open to the third floor. This afforded GSU a three-story system to manually store bulk freight indoors. The fourth and fifth stories were used for the automated ULD (Unit Load Device) container storage system. The building was on a corner of a taxiway. Aircraft used that taxiway to travel from one end of the airport to the various cargo buildings. As the aircraft passed the side of the building they would turn into the back for loading and offloading operations.

After Illya had cleared and prepared the back staging area behind the building for the arrival of URKRN, he went back into the break room for a cup of coffee. The other members of his crew were already there. The break room was in the back corner of the warehouse with a window facing the apron. A large table with chairs, one sofa and a TV made a comfortable place to take a lunch or coffee break.

The cargo supervisor briefed his men on the morning duties.

---

[5] Caster bed platforms able to transport 96 x 125 inch cargo pallets weighing 10,000 pounds.

"Once the aircraft has lowered its forward ramp, Boris will drive the earth mover on board." Looking down at his notes, the supervisor continued, "Illya, you and Dmytro will guide Boris in, and help secure the cargo. Any questions?"

"Who is working the rear of the aircraft?" Illya asked.

"That is not your problem. You just do your job and we will get this plane out on time and be drinking vodka by noon."

A moment later, they heard the roar of the massive engines as the aircraft turned into the back apron. Dmytro looked out the window. The loadmaster was guiding the aircraft into position. The wheels were chocked and the loadmaster crossed his arms in the air indicating to the pilot that the aircraft was secured and he could release the brake.

"They are just opening the nose of the aircraft. It will take another twenty minutes for it to kneel and extend the ramp. Plenty of time for another cup of coffee," a smiling Dmytro announced.

Twenty minutes later, the team ventured out onto the apron. Boris jumped onto the earthmover and turned the key. It did not start. He tried again and nothing. Illya jumped on the machine and shoved Boris over.

"Move over, babushka, and let a real man show you how it is done."

Illya turned the key and the engine roared. He smiled at Boris and jumped back down.

The earth mover began its trek up the ramp with Illya and Dmytro on each side, guiding Boris. Illya noticed the ULD's with the helicopters were still in the back of the aircraft. Finally, Boris was in position and Illya and Dmytro locked down the earthmover with heavy-duty tie-down straps wrapped around the axles and locked into the floor of the aircraft.

With everything loaded and locked in place, it was time to retrieve the document pouch. The pouch contained the necessary paperwork required for an international flight. This included the General Declaration form with the aircraft registration number, nationality, date, origin and destination. Included on the General Declaration were the names of all crew members, a declaration of health and the number of passengers on board, if any. Also included in the pouch were the cargo manifest, air waybills, and an international document for US Customs. In this case, because of the used earthmoving equipment, a Carnet for Temporary Admission of Goods into the United States had to be signed by a Ukrainian Customs officer before the aircraft left. The officer would verify that the item had left the country.

Thirty minutes later, the nose finally closed and the engines started. The loadmaster guided the pilot in turning the aircraft and then waved it off to airport ground control.

After cleaning the area, Illya took a break and walked to his car. He pulled out his cell and pressed one of his speed dial keys.

"Anna, I am sorry to wake you at such an early time but we have a problem. There was no switch. No ULDs were removed and none added, just the earthmover."

CHAPTER TWENTY

Saturday, 1:00 a.m. Local Time, JFK

There was no sense waking everyone at this hour. Anna decided to wait until 6 A.M. She was wondering how this would go over with York. He had not been impressed with her at yesterday's meeting. Now, he would never believe her. The rest of her night was restless. *How could I be so wrong? Our information was checked and double-checked!*

Finally, at 6 a.m., she made the call she dreaded.

"York."

"What is it Anna?"

"I am afraid we have made a mistake. It seems the LAW's are not on today's aircraft."

"What do you mean, not on **today's** aircraft?" Mike York snarled.

"I received a call at 1 a.m. My comrade in Kiev. He advised me they did not make any switch to the ULDs. The altered toy helicopters were not placed on board."

"Damn! We had everything planned. I have a staff meeting this morning to go over the action plan with my team."

"I know. I am sorry. I don't know what happened."

"Well, you better find out and let me know. How do I explain this to the Chief of Police? I look like an incompetent idiot."

"I will let you know what happened as soon as I find out. Will you call the rest of the team?"

"Yes, I was going to coordinate this anyway."

The call ended. Anna punched another call into her cell.

"Good morning, Anna."

"No, it's not. Moshe, the LAWs are not on board. I just had to tell Mike York and got my ass reamed, as they say here."

Anna described the 1 a.m. call from Illya. She repeated that the ULD's were not removed and replaced on the aircraft. Therefore, the LAWs were still in Kiev and now they had no idea where they were going to, or when.

"Do you expect to hear from Illya anytime soon?" Moshe inquired.

"Yes, I should hear from him today, one way or another."

"OK. Keep me informed."

"Of course. I think you are my only friend here now. Sorry."

Mike York now had to cancel his 11 a.m. meeting with his men. He took a moment and decided not to cancel it. He would use it as a briefing with his entire staff instead. They had not been together in one place for months. That would work.

Now for the daunting task of calling Steve Johnson at the FBI. This would be another awful call that had to be made. He went to his desk. Both hands were on top of his head as he leaned back in his chair, contemplating this next call. *I knew this was going to be a fiasco. Now I have to do the dirty work.*

"Steve Johnson here."

"Steve. It's Mike York."

"Hi Mike, what's up?"

"Apparently, nothing. I just got off the phone with Anna Sokolov. The whole thing is off."

"Why, what happened?"

"Nothing. The toy helicopters were not taken off and replaced for whatever reason. She doesn't know where they are now, or if they are coming here or not."

"You saw this coming, Mike. I can't change my people at this point, so I guess they're going to find out what manual labor is," said Steve with a hearty laugh.

"OK, I just wanted to let you know. Have a good day."

"Thanks, you too."

Saturday, 4:00 p.m. Local Time, Kiev

Illya's wife prepared his favorite dinner, a large kettle of borscht and, as usual, she made something extra for him to bring to work for lunch the next day.

Illya trudged through the front door and kissed his wife. "I smell borscht."

"Yes, and I made plenty. There will be extra for your lunch tomorrow."

"Great."

"Bring me your lunch bucket," she asked.

"Oh, I must have left it at work. Do I have time to get it?"

"Yes, but don't stop to talk to your friends."

Illya trotted out the door. Thirty minutes later, he pulled up to the building. He headed to the back of the building to the breakroom. As he picked up his lunch bucket, he noticed the men clearing the ramp behind the warehouse. He decided to go back and say hello to one of his friends on the second shift.

"Hello, Andriy, having a good night?" inquired Illya.

"Crazy, all the big shots are upstairs getting ready for some big dinner and just after you left we had another unscheduled plane leave."

"What flight was that?"

"It was an extra section, just a departure."

"Where was it going?"

"JFK! I don't know, it was here when I came in. It had the usual toy helicopters on board."

Illya walked away thinking, *is this the aircraft with the LAWs?* As he passed a trash dumpster he noticed something on the ground. He looked down. Decals. He picked one up and it read, **URKRN.** They had used decals to change the aircraft number.

"*Bozke mir*!" He yelled out as he slapped himself on the head.

Ukrainian borscht

Ingredients

1 cup of diced celery

1 cup of diced onions

1 cup of chopped cabbage

2 cloves of garlic, grated or pressed

1 tablespoon of butter (for sautéing onions and celery)

8 cups water or broth

1 can diced tomatoes (home or commercially canned)

3 medium to large-sized beets

1 or 2 medium carrots

1 medium potato

1/2 cup of fresh dill weed

Salt and pepper to taste

Optional ingredients: Green beans, peas, beet greens and shredded pork or pork sausage

Directions

1. Sauté the onions, celery and cabbage with the butter until soft and translucent. Then add the can of diced tomatoes and the garlic as well as all of the water or broth. Bring to a boil and then reduce to medium heat.

2. Peel the beets, carrots and potato. Then dice half the beets and grate the other half. Grate all the carrots. Dice the potato. Add all of these ingredients to the broth. If you would like to add any other optional vegetables (i.e., beans, peas, beet greens, etc.) do so now.

3. Allow soup to simmer on medium until diced beets and potatoes are soft (test them with a fork or by biting into them). Remove soup from heat.

4. Stir in chopped fresh dill weed and salt and pepper. Serve hot with a scoop of sour cream and a slice of bread and butter. Rye bread is best.

CHAPTER TWENTY-ONE

Saturday, 11:45 a.m. Local Time, JFK

Anna's phone began vibrating. She took a quick peek and noticed it was Illya.

"Yes, Illya, what did you find out?"

"The LAWs are on board the aircraft arriving at JFK **now.**"

"But, but, how could that happen?" Anna continued stuttering.

"The LAWs were already loaded on the aircraft here before my shift. The aircraft that I saw arrive never came to the apron that night. Instead there was another aircraft with the same registration numbers that pulled up to the apron behind the warehouse. That aircraft had been here already loaded with the LAWs, out of sight. I found decals in the trash with the same identification numbers. They switched aircraft on me."

"I must hang up. I have important calls to make." Anna shouted into the phone.

"Sorry." Illya replied and hung up.

Moshe was stationed on the back staging area, awaiting the aircraft. The pocket of Moshe's coveralls began to vibrate. He took a peek and saw Anna's name. He made a dash to the toilet holding his crotch. Everyone on the apron was laughing.

Inside the empty stall, he dialed Anna.

"Hurry. What is it?" Moshe whispered.

"The LAWs are on board. They switched aircraft. Can you stall the offload until the rest of the team get there?"

"I'll try."

"What did York say?"

"I hoped you would make that call."

"No problem."

Mike York had assembled his team at the JFK Postal Center and was in the middle of his prepared briefing. His cell rang. He looked down at the caller ID, *Moshe Kaplan. Now, what does he want?*

"Hello, Moshe, more bad news?" asked Mike, shaking his head back and forth.

"Mike, the LAWs are on board the aircraft. They switched aircraft in Kiev. The LAWs were already on board that aircraft when it left Kiev and it is now landing as we speak."

"Geez, how am I supposed to get my team there in time? What a fiasco."

"I'm trying to stall the offload," answered Moshe

"OK. Let me get on it. I have to call Steve at the FBI. Maybe his people can help stall the aircraft." He hung up.

Moshe ran outside and located the excavation company driver, displayed his identity badge, and told him to disappear and get some coffee. The driver ran back to his truck and drove away.

For the second time in the last twelve hours, York would call Steve Johnson.

"OK, what's it now."

"We're back on. Can you get hold of your men?"

"Got it," was all Steve said as he disconnected the call.

The yellow Allied Fuel truck was traveling along the airport service road towards the cargo area. Fred's walkie talkie crackled on the secured frequency.

"Where are you guys?" asked Steve.

"On the service road heading to the cargo area. What's up?"

"We're back on. Can you delay the aircraft from being off loaded?"

"Do what I can," Fred answered.

"Copy that," said Thomas, as he pulled the blue Triangle Maintenance step van out of the maintenance yard.

The lumbering colossal aluminum tube's shadow passed over the automobiles driving along Rockaway Boulevard, their drivers trying to get a glimpse of the huge aircraft as it passed what seemed to be no more than fifty feet above them. Songs on the car radios were drowned out by the tremendous roar from the four massive engines. Finally, there was the screech of the twenty-four huge tires as they touched down on runway 22L.

Airport control authorized flight YB450, aircraft **URKRN**, to taxi to cargo area D.

Five minutes passed as the aircraft approached the GSA back apron. Thomas and Fred pulled up to the apron and parked. They got out of their vehicles. Casually, they walked around their trucks. Fred opened the hood of his truck and started to examine the engine. He pulled out the 20 AMP fuel pump fuse.

"Hey, what's going on here? Move it. You're blocking my aircraft," yelled out the loadmaster, "I have an aircraft to park."

"OK! I'm moving. Didn't know you needed the whole back apron." Fred responded.

Slowly and precisely, Fred and Thomas got back into their trucks. Thomas started his engine and waited for Fred.

Fred slammed the hood down on his van and got in. A smirk came over Fred's face as his engine sputtered and stalled, but did not start. He tried cranking it over once again. But again, it just sputtered and stalled.

"What's wrong, now?" yelled the loadmaster.

"It won't start." Fred yelled back.

The loadmaster opened the hood and told Fred to try again. Meanwhile, Thomas had gotten out of his van and was now standing beside the loadmaster.

"What the fuck are you doing here? Get back in the fuckin' van and move it," he screamed.

"OK. Hold your water. I was just trying to help," Thomas answered as he slowly stepped back into the van.

The aircraft was now stationary just beyond the building.

Pavio was in his office waiting for the aircraft to turn the corner and park. He folded his arms in anticipation. There was a slight fluttering in his chest. He looked out the window just in time to see the loadmaster arguing with Fred. His head turned toward his desk and he looked at his computer. He thought back to last week with Holly. *That was a perplexing encounter. Could there be a connection with the commotion going on outside?* Pavio opened his desk drawer. There, on top of some papers was his Beretta. He packed the pistol under his GSA uniform jacket. Pavio's face turned flush. He stormed out of the office and ran out the back door. Standing nose to nose with Fred, he reached behind himself and pulled out the Beretta.

"If you don't get this fucking piece of shit off my ramp this minute, I will put this up your ass and blow your balls off," Pavio whispered in a menacing voice.

Once again, Fred opened the hood and this time replaced the fuel pump fuse.

Fred jumped back into the truck and the engine started. As he pulled away he yelled back to Pavio, "You'll hear from my union about this."

The loadmaster continued parking the aircraft. Finally, he crossed his hands above his head as the wheels were chocked and the pilot released the brake. Mobile stairs were rolled out to the aircraft, and the door opened. The pilot and his crew came out and walked down the steps. After waving to the loadmaster, they continued into the warehouse to the break room for a cup of coffee. Soon the van from the hotel would arrive with the outbound crew and they would be able to get some much-needed rest.

The loadmaster climbed up the stairway and entered the aircraft. After a few moments the nose of the plane started opening, revealing the huge cavern. Next, the nose wheel hydraulics started pulling the wheels back into the fuselage. The plane was now kneeling. A ramp began to extend from the front of the aircraft, revealing the massive earthmover.

Precious moments passed waiting for the certified heavy-duty machinery driver to move the earthmover, but no one arrived.

Pavio was screaming, "Get this fuckin' thing off my aircraft."

Moshe was happy to oblige and strutted up the ramp and climbed aboard the earthmover. Two other GSA warehouse personnel joined him and started releasing the tie-down straps. After the earthmover was free, Moshe started the engine and began driving the earthmover off the aircraft. The other two descended to the bottom of the ramp to guide him down.

Alexi climbed aboard the heavy-duty forklift and prepared to remove the ULD of LAWs once the earthmover was parked by the side of the warehouse.

Slowly, Moshe started the earthmover. He was almost at the bottom of the ramp when he made a sharp right and the front of the machine hit the ground. It was now jammed, hanging off the ramp.

Pavio's face was on fire. He rushed to the site of the accident, screaming.

"*Bozhe mir*, imbecile, get off the fuckin' machine," shouted Pavio to Moshe.

He continued to shout, now at Alexi, "Get your thumb out of your ass and move that thing immediately, before I make you another asshole," pointing to the earthmover.

Thomas and Fred were parked next to each other, watching from their vehicles, waiting for the SWAT team.

"That's our man. He must be the one Johnson told us not to shoot," remarked Thomas.

"I love it! He does good work," Fred replied trying to hold back his laughter.

Suddenly, sirens wailed. All heads turned toward the taxiway leading to the back apron, as flashing lights appeared. Everyone scattered, like a nest of mice startled by the cat.

Alexi freed the forklift and drove it around the far side of the building away from the arriving SWAT team. Pavio started to follow with Moshe in pursuit.

Moshe yelled out, "Pavio! Stop! Police!"

Pavio turned and pulled out his Beretta and fired two rounds, one hitting Moshe. Moshe fell to the ground, blood dripping from his left leg. He raised himself onto one knee and finally stood just in time to see Pavio turn the corner. Again, he took up the chase, only this time hobbling. Two more shots were fired as he reached the corner of the building. He turned. Pavio was pinned to the wall. His face was slack-jawed. His gun lay on the ground. A forklift blade protruded from his abdomen. Blood spurted onto the pavement, his head slumped over.

Still sitting on the forklift was Alexi. The two shots Pavio fired into Alexi's chest were his final act. Alexi was still alive but oozing blood. He looked up as Moshe approached.

"Moshe, he killed my little brother. Make them pay, all of them."

"I will, I promise."

EPILOGUE

Saturday, 2:00 p.m.

Anna had just hung up on the call from Moshe. She sat down and took a deep breath. She was finally able to calm down, now that the operation had been a success and the LAWs confiscated. She still wondered about the Kiev operation. The answer came within minutes. There, on her cell phone, were photos of all the players as they were arrested in Kiev during their dinner. The last photo was a smiling Illya with a thumbs up.

4:00 p.m., 100 Oak Drive, Port Jefferson, New York

A cab pulled up to the front of the house. The back door opened. The passenger lifted his leg, the one with the bandage, and placed it on the ground. With the help of the door, he lifted himself out of the car. He turned and grabbed his crutches from the back seat.

"Wait for me. I may be awhile. Is that OK?"

"Sure," answered the taxi driver.

Moshe hobbled up the path to the front door and rang the doorbell. Holly opened the door, her eyebrows went up as her jaw dropped.

"I'm fine. Are you going to let me in, or do I have to stand here all day?" Moshe asked, trying to steady his crutches.

She took him by his arm and helped him to the wing chair in the living room. She placed an ottoman under his legs.

"Comfy?"

"Quite."

"Looks like we have two cripples to take care of," said Jeff standing with his walker.

"I'm OK," Moshe continued, "how about you?"

"I'm fine. I'll be a little dizzy for the next few days, so the doc suggested this walker."

John ran up to Moshe, "So! What happened today?"

"Jeff is safe. Pavio deliberately crashed into the jet ski. Stepan overheard the plans to sell the LAWs and was upset. Mykhailo Chernov ordered Pavio to scare Stepan, but he went too far."

"Would you like something to drink?" offered Pat.

"Just black coffee, if you have it."

"Continue, please. What happened to you?" asked an anxious Holly.

When Moshe was finished describing what had happened in detail to the family, he explained that Alexi couldn't let Stepan's murder go. They were like brothers. He was just waiting for the right time and that was it. Before he died he made me promise to make them all pay. I did."

"What about the rest of them?" John asked.

"Well, Interpol is rounding up all the others in Kiev. They will spend the next 100 years in the gulag," Moshe continued, "here in your country it is quite different. Not so easy. But, Mykhailo is spending the weekend in jail. I was assured by your FBI that there would be no extradition, as they consider this an act of terrorism. He will be spending the rest of his life in prison."

John came out of the kitchen with five glass tumblers and a bottle of Jameson Irish Whiskey. "I think this calls for a drink," he said as he started pouring.

"None for me. I'm heavily medicated," stated Moshe.

"Then just a sip," answered John as he covered the bottom of Moshe's glass.

"Really? John," said Moshe

"To a job well done and happier days to follow," said John, as he finished off his drink.

The rest followed suit except Moshe who just looked at it.

"I stopped by to say goodbye to you all," said Moshe.

"Where are you going?" Pat asked.

"Back to Israel."

He started to get up, and Holly came to his aid. He kissed Pat on the cheek, and shook hands with John. Jeff pushed Moshe's hand away and gave him a hug. "I owe you my life."

Holly escorted Moshe to his waiting taxi.

"Do you really have to leave so soon?"

"*Malyshka*, it's time. My flight to Tel Aviv leaves at 11 p.m.

"But why tonight?"

"My identity has been compromised. There will be news photographers looking for me. I cannot let that happen. I must always be in the shadows." He paused, then continued, "Come with me. This is my last assignment. I'm retiring."

"No. I can't. Not yet. I have a dream too," she answered, tears welling.

"What's that?"

"I want to be a curator for a museum. That's why I went back to college.

"Here. This is my private cell phone number. If you ever visit Tel Aviv, call me. Most of all, if you ever need my help again, call me."

She looked at the card, *David Jordan, 972-3-555-0101.*

"Who is this?"

"Holly, my name isn't Moshe Kaplan, it's David Jordan."

"Who are you?"

"I'm Dav….."

"No! **Who** are you?"

"All I can tell you is I'm a captain in the Israeli Special Services."

"You lied to me and my family? Why?"

"It's my job. I lead a life of lies and deceit. Believe me I wanted to tell you since the first night we made love. I couldn't put you above the mission…"

"There was too much at stake. I would have placed you and your family in jeopardy."

"I sensed there was something from the beginning…" Holly turned away. Tears flooded her eyes. "Will I ever see you again?"

Moshe stepped closer and embraced Holly. He whispered, "I do care for you…so much…it's not a way of life for you."

He caressed her cheek and brushed back her hair. "Let's give it time."

Holly looked up at Moshe. They kissed farewell.

VOCABULARY

Russian words

Babushka: in Russian "old woman"; in English, a type of scarf commonly worn by a babushka.

Beluga: a type of whale or sturgeon.

Bolshevik: a revolutionary or radical, from the name of the majority Communist faction in Tsarist Russia, ultimately from the Russian word for "majority."

Bozke mir: God Damm.

Malyshka: Babe.

Ruble: the basic unit of the Russian currency.

Troika: a carriage or sleigh pulled by three horses or a triumvirate (a ruling or administrative trio).

Ushanka: a fur cap with ear flaps.

CAST OF CHARACTERS
Order of Appearance

Jeff Flynn: Driver of Jet Ski

Stepan Bondar: Jeff Flynn's friend.

Pavio Kravets: Captain in New York's Russian Mafia

Mike Foster: Sergeant Suffolk County Marine Police

Dale Thomas: Suffolk County Police Chief

John Flynn: Jeff's father

Danielle McGregor: Charge Nurse

Holly Flynn: Jeff's older sister

Pat Flynn: Jeff's mother

Anna Bondar: Stepan's wife

Alexi Danko: Stepan's friend and coworker

Mykhailo Chernov: Head of the New York Russian Mafia

Moshe Kaplan Holly Flynn's love interest

Susan Shepard: Suffolk County District Attorney

Samuel Baum: Jeff's Lawyer

Vasili Petrov: Head of Russian Mafia

Ivan Kushnir: Head of Ukrainian Mafia

Michael York: NYPD Emergency Services Unit (ESU)

Steven Johnson: Special Agent FBI

Anna Sokolov: Detective Chief Superintendent Interpol

Illya Kozlov: Interpol undercover agent at cargo operations in Kiev

BIBLIOGRAPHY

www.theatlantic.com   The Mossad

www.wikipedia.org   Soviet-Afghan War

University of California Press - A Client Government in Afghanistan
https://publishing.cdlib.org/ucpressebooks

www.ingramcontent.com/pod-product-compliance
Lightning Source LLC
Chambersburg PA
CBHW020640180626
46816CB00003B/1062